HARPERVIA

An Imprint of HarperCollins*Publishers*

COUNTER-
ATTACKS
AT THIRTY

A NOVEL

COUNTER-ATTACKS AT THIRTY

WON-PYUNG SOHN

TRANSLATED BY SEAN LIN HALBERT

COUNTERATTACKS AT THIRTY. Copyright © 2017 by Won-pyung Sohn. English Translation Copyright © 2025 by Sean Lin Halbert. All rights reserved. Printed in the United States of America. No part of this book may be used or reproduced in any manner whatsoever without written permission except in the case of brief quotations embodied in critical articles and reviews. For information, address HarperCollins Publishers, 195 Broadway, New York, NY 10007.

HarperCollins books may be purchased for educational, business, or sales promotional use. For information, please email the Special Markets Department at SPsales@harpercollins.com.

Originally published as *Seoreunui bangyeok* in South Korea in 2017 by EunHaengNaMu.

FIRST HARPERVIA HARDCOVER PUBLISHED IN MARCH 2025

Designed by Yvonne Chan

Library of Congress Cataloging-in-Publication Data has been applied for.

ISBN 978-0-06-337810-0
ISBN 978-0-06-343747-0 (ANZ)
ISBN 978-0-06-342478-4 (Intl)

25 26 27 28 29 LBC 5 4 3 2 1

CONTENTS

1

BORN 1988

The year I was born, there was a man with a large nose living in South Korea. White-haired and a retired general, he lived a life that was as far from ordinary as you could get. But then just before turning sixty, the words "ordinary people" suddenly became one of his favorite phrases. He liked this phrase so much that he started to introduce himself as an "ordinary person," always remembering to follow this self-proclamation with "Trust me," as if he knew people wouldn't. He even started going around claiming that the "era of ordinary people" was coming. Thus, it was to everyone's surprise that he used this script-flipping slogan to rise to the highest office in Korea. But the *un*ordinary trajectory of his life didn't stop there. Most famously, a picture of him and the previous president standing shoulder to shoulder, handcuffed and dressed in blue prison uniforms, made the front page of every newspaper in Korea. You would be hard-pressed to find an ordinary person who had experienced the things he had.

Even though this all happened around the time of my birth,

I knew it like I'd experienced it firsthand. The rest of his story, however—the protests, the fighting, the bloodshed in the square—were nothing to me but tales from long ago, things I had to learn about through books and documentaries. Since then, the world has taken a few steps in the right direction—but only a few. Injustice is still the law of the land, and the promised era of ordinary people never came. What we got instead was the exact opposite: a world in which ordinary people are forced to follow the crowd while simultaneously being expected to use every method to stand out from it, desperately screaming at the tops of their lungs, begging to be noticed. As for me, I am just one of the many unfortunate souls whose farewell to youth came during this era.

Of course, I have my own unique origin story. And like most people born under unique circumstances, my mom loves telling everyone she meets about how I came into this world. So whenever the topic of how I got the name Jihye comes up, she tells a tale that starts one sultry summer day in 1988 with a lonesome boy rolling a hoop across a sports field in Seoul. Fascinated by the story of a developing country hosting the Olympics, the whole world was watching with anticipation. Likewise, every Korean was glued to their television set, white-knuckled and praying that a mere boy, barely seven years old, could roll a hoop across the world's biggest stage without messing up.

For the rest of the games, that video of the Hoop Boy, as he came to be known, was replayed on proud news channels across the peninsula. Every night, our small apartment complex in Junggye-dong was filled with cheers of joy and groans of disappointment as people watched the festivities.

One afternoon, my mom was watching the games on TV, her

body sprawled out on the couch. She rested one hand on her bulging stomach as she used the other to desperately fan fresh air toward her face—despite it being late September, the summer heat had yet to leave the city. Her eyebrows were pulled up to the middle of her forehead in anger as she thought about my dad, who'd stayed out late the previous night drinking. But on a deeper level, her mind was perturbed by the name the baby in her stomach would take when born.

It was destiny that I be named Chu-bong (秋峰). Constructed from two Chinese characters that meant autumn and mountain peak, the name could be interpreted as "peak of autumn" or "the pinnacle of beauty." But unlike its beautiful meaning, the name itself sounded hideous, like it belonged to an old man. Not surprisingly, it had been carefully selected by my grandfather, who had taught Confucian classics in the North before coming down as a refugee during the war. Because my dad's generation was the third consecutive generation in his family with only one son, and because his father had lived such a hard life as a refugee from the North, he had no intention of disobeying his father's wishes and giving in to my mother's sulking.

When she first heard the news that the child in her stomach was to receive the hideous name Chu-bong, she fell into despair and spent several sleepless nights with tears in her eyes. She pleaded with him to change the name, but my dad wouldn't budge. The best he could offer her were a few reluctant words of consolation:

"You should consider yourself lucky that the baby will be born in the fall. Can you imagine if it were born in the spring? Then its name would be *Chun*-bong. That sounds even worse. And thank goodness my last name isn't Koh. *Kim* Chu-bong is one hundred times better than *Koh Chu*-bong."

It took my mom a second to understand what he meant, but as soon as she recognized the double entendre of "Koh Chu"—which in Korean meant both pepper and penis—she burst into tears again. Realizing he'd only made things worse, my dad excused himself with a fake cough and distanced himself from her sobs.

Because my mom had been given the name Bae Mal-suk, which was a common yet old-fashioned name for someone born in the early 1960s, she had always had the dream of giving her child a beautiful name. But now all she could do was pray that the child in her stomach wasn't a girl.

On the TV, Carl Lewis and Ben Johnson were just about to face off in the 100-meter final. My mom had been sensing a disturbance in her stomach for some time now, but her mind was too preoccupied to notice that the pain was coming in regular intervals. She picked at the calluses on her fingertips, filled with resentment toward my dad and repeating to herself the name that her baby would have to carry for life. As soon as my grandpa had heard the news that his daughter-in-law was pregnant, he pulled out a calendar, calculated the month I would be born, and then wrote down my name on a notepad. That piece of paper became his last will and testament because, just a few days later, he passed away. Had he lived just a bit longer, my mom might have been able to negotiate with him, but instead he died suddenly, leaving behind nothing but that cursed will. Just thinking about this and the fact that her husband had left her home alone when she was due any day, and with no way for her to contact him, was enough to make her break out in tears again.

It was at that exact moment that the contractions started in full force. With shaky hands, she left a note for my dad that was written much nicer than how she truly felt:

4

—*I'm headed to the hospital. Please hurry. The baby is coming.*

After barely managing to get herself out of the house, she waited on the street for a long time before she finally caught a cab that drove her safely to the hospital. Just as the pain was starting to become unbearable, my dad appeared, ruddy from trying to cure his hangover with yet more alcohol.

Even as she howled like an animal in agony, my mom did her best to give him a death glare. Ashamed and embarrassed, he said in a halting voice the only thing he could think of to say:

"I heard Ben Johnson won."

The slap that my mom gave him right after he said this was the first and last time she ever hit him.

My mother's long, painful labor continued, but for some reason, I refused to come out. Perhaps it was because I'd grown attached to my mother's womb, which I'd called home for the last nine months; perhaps it was because I hated the name Chu-bong; or perhaps it was simply because I was afraid of the world I'd have to face.

After two days of excruciating pain, my mom's face was pale and gaunt. But when the doctor suggested surgery, my mom refused. She said the baby wasn't coming out until its mother had what she wanted. It seemed my mom had realized that she had leverage over the situation. Dumbfounded, the doctor said he'd never seen such an obstinate woman. My dad, on the other hand, said nothing and merely looked down at his feet. Eventually, the doctor fixed his glasses and said, "At this rate, both the mother and child could die." It was then that she presented my dad with an ultimatum:

"I'd rather die than name my child Chu-bong. I want your word."

My dad's face was pale white as he decided between his late

father and pregnant wife. In the end, he decided to save the living. He turned to her and nodded with conviction. Barely conscious and with the help of the doctor's hand, my mother wrote a memorandum.

"Remember this. If you go behind my back and use the name your father made, I'll take the child and never return. I swear."

Just before she went into the operating room, a sign came. My mom let out a few short, intense breaths to psych herself up, just like she'd read about in a book. And after just three of these, I came into the world. A baby girl. Thinking about how close her daughter had been to being named Kim Chu-bong, she held me close as she cried tears of relief and joy.

A few hours after taking my first breath, I fell into a peaceful sleep. And that night, as if to symbolize my mother's comeback victory, the gold medal in the men's 100-meter final was stripped from Ben Johnson and handed to Carl Lewis. At the same time, my mom, who must have been tired from her long, tear-filled battle and who hadn't finished her postpartum care, stayed up all night flipping through the pages of a Chinese character dictionary searching for my name. What she settled on was the most common name for girls born in Korea in 1988: Kim Jihye.

Although the story of how I got my name was as spectacular as the battle between Carl Lewis and Ben Johnson, everything else related to my name was completely *un*spectacular.

On the first day of elementary school when my teacher called out my name, another girl answered before me. Her name, it turned out, was also Kim Jihye. Awhile later, my teacher called my name again, but this time, too, another girl beat me to the punch. Eventually I realized that my name was written on the attendance sheet as "Kim Jihye 3."

Things like this happened throughout grade school. Wherever I went, there was always a handful of Kim Jihyes; the only difference was what the teacher decided to attach to our names. When we started learning English, 123 became ABC. And one year in middle school, I was in a class with four other Kim Jihyes. It was pure chaos. Numbers and letters weren't going to cut it. Our teacher decided on adjectives: Big Kim Jihye, Little Kim Jihye, Fair-skinned Kim Jihye, Tan Kim Jihye, and even Chubby Kim Jihye. Indeed, more than our names, it was these modifiers that distinguished us. I was given what I considered to be the least interesting descriptor: Little Kim Jihye. But I didn't receive this designation because I was particularly small or petite; it was just that Big Kim Jihye was so much larger than me. So naturally, as the most average of all the Kim Jihyes, I had to be Little Kim Jihye. And Jihye wasn't the only absurdly common name in Korea that year. Just as common were the girl names Minji, Eunji, Eunjeong, and Hyejin. Slightly less common, but still common enough to have at least one instance in every class—like a smattering of sprinkles on ice cream—were the names Boram, Areum, and Seulgi. Anyway, that was how all the Jihyes of Korea grew up: as friends with all the other Minjis, Eunjis, Eunjeongs, Hyejins, Borams, Areums, and Seulgis of Korea.

Even outside of school, it was easy to find people with the same name as me. It was always problematic when the name Kim Jihye was pulled out of a hat for a prize raffle at cram school. And I often turned over bags of chips to see if the factory worker who packaged it had the same name as me. I even shared names with several celebrities—although all of them had changed their name to something less common. It was so bad that sometimes "Kim Ji-hye" felt more like a common noun, like dog or cat, than it did my own name. And yet, while I often lamented the commonness of my name, most of the time, its banality suited me. In fact, I was very grateful for the anonymity it provided me. It was a name fit for a person who didn't have much to brag about.

Of course, after failing countless job interviews, it stung when I realized the name on the acceptance list for the content planning department at DM Group (the company I really wanted to work at) belonged not to me but to another Kim Jihye. But because I was used to resignation, it didn't take long for me to convince myself that it just wasn't meant to be.

Just before racing Ben Johnson, Carl Lewis gave a bold prediction: "No man has ever run in front of me." In response to this, Ben Johnson said, "And I've never run with the intent of staring at someone's behind." But quotes like these weren't meant for people like me. If I were a runner, I would be a faceless marathon runner in the middle of the pack. Lost in a crowd and headed toward a destination I can't see as my lungs desperately search for oxygen, I'm frantically shuffling my feet, doing my best just not to fall below the median line. But I think it's fortunate that this isn't particularly tragic, that I can sometimes form a confident smile on my face.

Anyway, that is how I came to be the person I am today.

THE CRY

"eong, Yeon, same difference," Team Leader Yu muttered in annoyance as she sat next to me.

She was on the phone with a student, confirming receipt of their tuition payment, when she accidentally called the student Choi Jae-yeon instead of Choi Jae-yeong, with a "g." It was for this reason that she was angrily muttering to herself like this. I simply picked up my stack of papers and left the office when she hung up, instead of pointing out that, when it came to someone's name, one letter made a huge difference.

Sitting in front of the window was a large copy machine. The old thing clashed with the new interior of the office, which had just been renovated—they hadn't swapped it out because it still worked, more or less. Operating at full autopilot, I opened the rickety scanner lid and began copying documents. The materials were for the lecture "Art and Philosophy," so naturally, I had a lot to get through.

Even the simplest task requires a bit of skill. For example, I would use a large book to cover the exposed bits of glass that the broken lid couldn't—the only way I could prevent the harsh lasers shooting out of the scanner from burning my retinas. And because I had a lot of material to copy every day, it was important that I preemptively refill the paper tray before it got too low; otherwise, I'd waste time clearing paper jams. One day, I decided to share my tricks for using the copy machine with Team Leader Yu. But all she said in response was, "It's just document scanning, Jihye. It shouldn't be that hard." She paused before giving me a look of pity and saying that I'd only have to suffer a bit longer, as we'd be getting the new copy machine soon. But I knew that easier jobs meant smaller jobs.

When I was young, there was this popular anti-joke about putting elephants in a fridge. The joke went like this: How do you put an elephant in a refrigerator? You open the door and put the elephant inside. No duh. Copying documents is the same deal; no need to overthink things. You open the lid, put the paper in, and press copy. It's an idiot-proof equation with clear causes and obvious results—the kind of equation where I don't exist as a variable.

Every time the gold light of the scanner passed across the skin of my cheek, the printer spat out the words of Aristotle and Plato. Apparently, Plato hated artists, and Aristotle barely tolerated them. Next were Andy Warhol's paintings of Campbell's chicken noodle soup and Marilyn Monroe's face. Is such art original or merely ready-made? Is art creation, or is it all imitation? What is the function of art? *Blah blah blah.* I'd taken electives like these when I was in college. But why? Why would anyone take classes like this? What application did such knowledge have to real life?

I turned to look out the window. There was a large tree just outside the glass; I was having trouble identifying what kind of tree it was because the leaves hadn't emerged yet. But more importantly, this was one of the few places in the office where I could look outside. The building wasn't a department store, and yet it barely had any windows. Perhaps it was because cultured people—you know, the kind who took a lot of electives in college—weren't meant to stare vacantly out windows.

After delivering the copied materials to the lecture hall, I returned to my desk and packed my bag. Just before leaving the office to run an errand for a professor, I turned to Team Leader Yu and asked in the most irritated voice I could manage, as if I hated being sent on ridiculous errands: "Do I really have to deliver this in person?"

"That's just what I'm talking about, Jihye—" Team Leader Yu began as soon as I was finished. "It's times like this where you show just how maladjusted you are. Look, I'm tired of explaining everything to you. Just think of this as a chance to stretch your legs and get some fresh air."

My simple strategy had worked. Although it was a nuisance having to use my head for something so trivial, at least this way Team Leader Yu wouldn't think I was enjoying myself while everyone stacked chairs.

Team Leader Yu was eleven years my senior and had been here longer than anyone. Her claim to fame was that she once persevered through an entire presentation after her water broke, successfully convincing a foreign pop star to bring their international tour to Korea. One time, I asked sarcastically how someone with such an impressive resume ended up in a place like this.

"Someday you'll understand, Jihye," Team Leader Yu said with a long sigh. "Maybe after you get married and have two kids."

This was one of Team Leader Yu's favorite responses. "You can't understand if you haven't had kids." Indeed, as a woman, she'd had a tough time working her way up the corporate ladder, and it was this will to succeed that won her the admiration of all the old, conservative men in the company. She was also extremely territorial, always reminding people of her rank and accomplishments. Her worldview as someone who suffered for many years before finally making it had made her a hard boss to talk to. So, if I wanted to be somewhat comfortable around her, I had to use my head at least a little, if not as much as she did. As a lowly intern in her thirties, I had no choice but to copy her every move, no matter how much it pained me to do so.

I exited the office building and boarded a bus across the street. Even though I commuted to the same building every day, it'd been forever since I'd gazed from afar at my workplace like this. The name DIAMANT was embossed on the side of the building. Most Koreans would read it as dye-ah-muhnt, not dee-ah-mon as the French word for "diamond" was supposed to be pronounced. Indeed, while everyone had heard of DM Group, few knew DM stood for Diamant. Somehow, its abbreviation had supplanted the original name. Of course, I wondered whether it was correct to abbreviate a single word with two letters like this, but perhaps they had no choice once they'd registered a one-word company name.

The success story of DM Group, which started off as a concrete company and later expanded to everything from construction and electronics to makeup and education, was no different from any of the other large conglomerates of South Korea. If there was a difference, it would be that DM had jumped into the culture industry much earlier than the others. It was because of this that its influence on, or rather, its stake in the South Korean culture industry was so huge. True to its name, everything that Diamant touched—movies, plays, music, food—sparkled and shined. Most distinguished and unique of all its subsidiaries was the education-focused Diamant Academy. Rumor had it that the company's founder, who never graduated elementary school, had an inferiority complex regarding his education. I guess the academy was the physical manifestation of his unfulfilled desire for a proper education.

The academy was located in a back alley of Jushin-dong, far away from the other subsidiaries, which were all located in and around Gangnam. The neighborhood had once been one of Seoul's famous shantytowns, but several parts of the area had been targeted by redevelopment projects in the '70s, so now the region was punctuated with bald patches of empty lots, between which neglected, old apartment buildings jutted out of the earth like lone steeples. Against this backdrop of poverty was a singularly glorious building reaching up toward the sky: Diamant Academy.

At the top of the ivory-colored building was a signboard bedazzled with large pearl or diamond-like beads. It sparkled and shined whenever it received the sunlight, but on rainy or overcast days, it had an oddly somber and oppressive feeling to it. Today, thankfully, the whole building was dancing with sunlight. In fact, the reflections were so intense that you could hardly read the sign without squinting. It looked just like the kind of ivory tower a large conglomerate would erect. People came here to be cultured. The curriculum of Diamant Academy, which distinguished itself from culture centers through its emphasis on the liberal arts, boasted courses in everything from beginning Latin to modern French philosophy.

Entering the DM Group through an internship at the academy was a scheme I'd cooked up once I failed to get hired through DM Group's official hiring channels. I thought I'd be able to transfer to headquarters if I first built up my resume as an intern-turned-full-time employee. But *when* would that happen? The bus made a large turn and started heading downtown.

I went into the Coffee Bean, which was located along Gwanghwamun Dae-ro, the giant road that leads up to the entrance of Gyeongbok-gung Palace. It was early February, when the only talk about the arrival of spring was from fashion brands and other advertisements. The air was still chilly. I rested my chin on my hand and looked out the window. In the gaps between pedestrians dressed in thick coats, I caught glimpses of yellow forsythia. I pitied the little flowers, which were bearing the brunt of freezing temperatures and harsh winds. They must have come out thinking it was spring—last week, there had been three days of unseasonably warm weather. Now that they were out and blooming, they'd probably all freeze to death, I guessed. Death aside, I was taken aback by their yellowness, which was bright enough to hurt my eyes. They're the only ones in this entire city of gray that feel alive. What were they trying to prove?

I looked at the time once my silent prayer for the forsythia was over. Professor Park was already fifteen minutes late for our meeting, and hadn't mentioned to anyone that he might run late. Then again, he wasn't coming here to see me; he was coming here to receive the thing I'd brought for him.

Our academy was riding the wave of a recent boom of interest in the liberal arts, and Professor Park Chang-sik was our hottest commodity. Thanks to his runaway bestseller, *Eroticism and Love*, which borrowed the name of a course he'd taught back when he was a professor at the university, his lectures always had at least seventy students. Because of this, they probably felt less like real classes and more like a series of special lectures given by a celebrity, and yet, this never seemed to deter any prospective students.

I was appalled last winter when I TA'ed for his class for the first time. Each week, I was required to make copies of pornographic photos from cultures all over the world and play video recordings of humans and other mammals having sex (sometimes together) for the students. The bulk of his lectures revolved around explaining the philosophy and aesthetics behind these sexual acts. Looking at erotic materials for work was one thing, but listening to the groaning and moaning of humans and animals in a room filled with other adults was beyond bearable. As soon as I set up the projector and pressed play, I was out of there.

I couldn't believe my eyes when I finally gave his bestseller a read. He hadn't changed a single word between his book and his lecture notes. No additional remarks, no variation. He literally delivered his lectures as if he were reading from the book. The only thing that was different was that the pictures could now be appreciated in their original high-def resolutions. And yet, his lectures remained popular. According to Team Leader Yu, reading his book verbatim *was* the secret.

"Creativity hurts the brain, Jihye. All people want is to experience famous things for themselves and feel like they've understood it. People feel good about themselves when they've experienced something firsthand that they think is highbrow. And then they spread the word by bragging about it on Instagram. That's marketing at its finest."

15

I took out the long, thin, black machine from my bag and placed it on the table. An iPhone 7 Plus. This little device was the reason for my existence right now. Professor Park had left his cell phone in class. He called and brazenly said that he didn't have the time to come back and demanded someone bring it to him. Thanks to this unexpected errand, I was able to have some peaceful afternoon time outside of the office.

His phone, whose contract probably hadn't been paid off yet, was shiny with oil and fingerprints. I had a sneaking suspicion that this little black box was filled with all sorts of kinky pornography, everything ranging from your run-of-the-mill girl-on-girl action to the really weird stuff like bestiality. I tried to erase the debauched images from my mind as I quietly sipped on my latte.

Spending a weekday afternoon like this gave me the illusion that I was a woman of leisure. I'd been to this café many times before. Back when I was still unemployed, I would buy a coffee and spend all day working on job applications. At lunchtime, people in suits and wearing company badges around their necks would flood the café. The simple fact that these people worked in skyscrapers in the heart of the city filled my eyes with envy. But that's why I came here; I wanted to be motivated. So, convinced that someday I'd be just like them, I would sit there all day sipping cold coffee as I studied for the TOEIC, edited personal statements, and practiced answering interview questions until my lips were dry.

I was lost in thought when Professor Park opened the door and entered the café. He looked impatient and inconvenienced. I stood up to bring attention to my insignificant existence. It was then that a sudden, loud voice—almost a cry—filled the café.

"Professor Park!"

That cry signaled the beginning of everything that was to come.

* * *

Deep and bassy, the voice was loud enough to attract the attention of everyone in the café. Professor Park and I, and everyone else in the café turned our gazes toward the source of the voice. There, standing in the corner of the café, a good fifteen meters from Professor Park, and coincidentally at the table right next to me, was a man.

"Downloading pornography from foreign websites and selling them as lectures. Aren't you embarrassed of yourself?"

The man barked this question. I looked up at him in shock as I distanced myself so that people wouldn't think we were together. He looked like a mountain bandit, an appearance that went well with his earthy voice. He had a bushy beard that wrapped itself around his chin and a full head of disheveled hair. But in contrast to his somewhat brutish size, he had a pointy nose and sharp jawline. In an instant, the café had become silent, as though it had been submerged in water.

Professor Park lifted his glasses and squinted as he tried to make out the man's face. I sat back down in my chair while trying not to draw attention to myself.

"Have we—?" The professor's voice trembled slightly.

"Have we met? Don't tell me you've already forgotten. I'm the part-time employee who worked for you when you were writing your book. You never paid me for running all your errands. And then you submitted the manuscript *I* wrote to the publisher without crediting me. Is selling foreign pornography to students not enough for you? Is that why you had to also exploit your assistant, too? Have you no shame? And whatever happened to those charges? You know, the ones about your having sex with a minor."

The man said all of this in one go, as though he had memorized a script. The people in the café stared at him without moving. The café worker nearest us, who was holding an empty tray under her arm, was exchanging urgent glances with the other employees.

The professor's face slowly lost its color, except for his forehead, which with its receding hairline was turning bright red, making it look like he had on a cap. He looked flustered, but he was standing too far away from the man to defend himself without raising his voice.

"You wait and see. You can't keep running from the shame. One day, it'll catch up with you."

And with that, the man stormed out of the café as he kicked up a violent gust of wind. I could see people starting to whisper among themselves. The professor stood there for a moment, frozen in place as though someone had pulled the plug. But, jolted back to life by the stares of people in the café, his body started to shake. When he finally snapped out of his trance, he turned around and walked out of the café. I chased after him. I still needed to give him back his cell phone. He was standing outside the café, slightly bent over and wiping the perspiration from his forehead.

"Hi, Professor."

I smiled and handed him his device as though I'd seen nothing.

"I've never! Is that how you young people act these days? No wonder!"

The professor raised his voice and shook his finger at me as if I were the man from earlier. I let out a faint sigh as I raised my eyebrows, meant to indicate "I don't know what you're talking about and I'm not interested"—an effective method, when used at the right time, for dealing with people who were on a tirade. After all, snapping back at him and telling him politely to shut up was above my pay grade.

The professor seemed too riled up to sense my small act of defiance, and simply repeated to himself a bunch of "I've nevers"s and "Who does he think he is?"s before turning to leave. In my head, I made a small bet with myself about whether he'd say thank you. I'll leave the results of the wager up to your imagination.

I went back into Coffee Bean and sat down. I didn't want to risk the possibility of running into Professor Park again by leaving immediately. I only got up from my seat after fifteen minutes of dawdling and flipping through a magazine. When I checked my phone, I had eight unread KakaoTalk messages from Team Leader Yu. I didn't open the app, but judging from the last notification, which read, "When are you coming back?," it was obvious what the other messages said. I thought to myself that I could use a dead cell phone battery as an excuse. As long as I left the little "1" next to the messages, which meant the recipient hadn't read them, I'd be safe.

I took the subway back home. I didn't know what the disturbance that afternoon meant. But the cry was enough to remind me of something I'd forgotten.

Twenty years ago, Professor Park, who'd been a professor of English literature at D University, was stripped of his position. It was because he'd (allegedly) had sex with a minor in the back of his car. While there were a lot of rumors about whether she was really a minor, in the end he didn't serve any time and only received two

19

years of probation. Of course, news of a professor at a prestigious university having sex with a minor made it impossible for the university not to fire him. And yet his life somehow kept going. In fact, it did more than that; he successfully made a comeback, becoming a bestselling author and celebrity lecturer. Even though he held no position at any college, everyone continued to call him Professor. Such was the world. I closed my eyes.

The train let out a roar as it accelerated. I tried to imagine which neighborhood we were passing beneath. Feeling the reverberations of the train as it slithered along, I thought about how I was a parasite meandering beneath the skin of the city. How many people on the surface, walking on the street or riding in their cars, thought about the thunderous electric locomotives racing beneath their feet? Even those who knew didn't act like they knew. They lived their lives as if they'd forgotten.

I opened my eyes, sensing someone coming toward me. I couldn't say I recognized him, but I felt like I'd seen his face many times. He squeezed his butt into the empty seat next to me before I had the chance to place his face. As the stranger leaned back and laid claim to more seat real estate, I realized who he was. The bearded man from the coffee shop, the one who'd sucker punched Professor Park with his insolent tongue!

The man took something out from inside of his jacket. It was one of those free newspapers they hand out at the entrances to subway stations. He noisily flipped through the paper for a while before rummaging through the clutter in his pocket for a pen. Once he found one, he began solving a crossword puzzle of Sino-Korean idioms derived from old tales. It was 2017, and he was still solving crosswords in the newspaper? Looking up at the man's reflection in the mirror across from us, I found that his appearance was hard to define in one word. Trying my best not to turn my head, I studied him out of the corner of my eye. His thick forearms were covered in hair. But the hair wasn't dense, so it wasn't particularly unsightly. Although he was big-boned and somewhat brutish, he had immaculate skin. His long, black eyelashes, which curled toward the skin slightly, would brush downward against his glasses like windshield wipers every time he blinked.

I silently observed him until he finished solving the crossword puzzle. His guesses were as follows:

Boil the dog after the rabbit hunt (兔死狗烹)
Nine deaths and still alive (九死一生)
Do something even if it kills you (死生決斷)
He who ties the knot must untie it (結者解之)
Noble and pure (至高至純)
Great sweetness follows great bitterness (苦盡甘來)

At the youngest, I'd guess he was thirty. And he probably didn't have a regular job, judging from the fact he was riding the subway on a Monday afternoon without even a bag. In fact, looking the way he did, he could pass for a struggling comic artist or some indie musician who frequented Hongdae. Then I thought of the incident from earlier, and I knew that he was probably going through hard times. As I continued to make conjectures about his identity, he turned the page to peruse the job postings, convincing me of his unemployment. There was a tattoo of a star on his thick-boned wrist. He was the kind of man you'd have a hard time forgetting.

I felt my cell phone vibrating in my bag. Team Leader Yu. I debated whether I should pick up but let it go to voicemail. In the meantime, the man had disappeared. I couldn't believe that such a large body could disappear so quickly without my noticing. Before long, the empty spot next to me was taken by another stranger. The number of unread messages from Team Leader Yu had ballooned to twenty-one. My phone continued to ding with KakaoTalk notifications: *ggaddok, ggaddok*. I could almost empathize with Team Leader Yu. The day I was dumped I stayed up all night desperately trying to make contact. More than two hundred messages sent, and not a single one read.

As the train slid toward the next subway station, I was already huddled close to the exit, clasping tightly to the silver handrail, which was dirty with oily fingerprints. I tensed my shoulders, which was the least I could do for my boss since I wasn't going to look at her angry messages.

3

MY FRIEND, MR. JEONG-JIN

eam Leader Yu welcomed me back to the office later that afternoon with a harsh scolding. She said she was disappointed because I wasted an entire day at work to finish just one small errand, but I knew the real reason was because I had left her to stack all the chairs by herself. Thou shalt not engage in physical labor—one of Team Leader Yu's unbreakable rules for life as a white-collared worker. This was also, in her mind at least, one of the key differentiating factors between her and non-regular workers, people whose employment status was temporary, provisional, probationary, subject to change at any moment, just like me, an intern.

That night, I came home and did an internet search with Professor Park's name. Most results were reviews raving about his lectures. There were a few news articles from twenty years ago about his unethical conduct involving a minor, but they weren't the type of stuff you could find without going out of your way to look for it. I kept digging and eventually discovered several online forums with long lists of people alleging he'd plagiarized grad students' research.

But this seemed like your typical student gossip, swept under the rug and not significant enough to harm his reputation. And recent posts were nonexistent. Suddenly, I was reminded of something the professor once said at an office dinner party.

"My lectures are like an apartment in Gangnam whose rent never goes up. Gosh, now that I think about it, I'm a magnanimous man, aren't I. Hahaha!"

It was through boastful comments like this that I first realized the professor considered himself a small celebrity. The point of this comment, in particular, was not just to brag, but also to request a raise. But despite what people might think, just because we belonged to a large conglomerate didn't mean we had that much funding. Thus, come spring semester, it was only natural that he made excuses to stop lecturing. But the fact that I'd been sent to return his cell phone to him in person—when he could have just as well come back to the office to get it himself—indicated that he was still influential. I closed the internet browser and the forgotten stories and rumors disappeared from sight.

I didn't mention what happened that day at Coffee Bean to anyone. I felt no ill will (or goodwill, for that matter) toward the professor, and preventing the spread of rumors was common decency. Plus, Team Leader Yu took pleasure in talking about people behind their back, and the last thing I wanted to do was enable a gossipmonger.

Above Team Leader Yu were Director Park, Deputy Department Head Yun, and Department Head Kim, none of whom I thought deserved their positions. Director Park, a journalist by trade, played the roles of poster boy and figurehead. And Deputy Department Head Yun, whom Director Park brought over with him from the newspaper, played the important role of "friend to the director."

As far as I saw it, the only things they did were talk about politics and the stock market, play Go, and kiss ass whenever an influential person visited the academy.

The only one of the three who did any work was Dept. Head Kim. He was the one who made the consequential decisions, who saw to daily operations and reported to HQ, who gave orders to everyone below him. And although there were two other team leaders besides Team Leader Yu, namely marketing and accounting, it was between Dept. Head Kim and Team Leader Yu that all the work got done. It was somewhat of a broken system, but it worked because we were a small academy. Besides, with industries like movies and food and produce to worry about, HQ couldn't spare much attention to the deformed and unwanted child that was Diamant Academy.

* * *

In Korea, places for learning come alive in the spring. Schools start their academic years abuzz with energy from the Lunar New Year and Samiljeol, the yearly celebration of the March First Independence Movement. And Diamant Academy was no exception. Eager students rushed to the academy in March with New Year's resolutions to learn something and improve their lives. It was also the period in which the academy did its yearly shuffling. When I heard that they weren't going to bring any employees over from HQ for a while, inside my head, I wondered if that meant they planned to hire me as a regular employee, and spent several days half filled with expectation, half filled with anxiety.

I was just reaching the nine-month mark from when I'd started working here as an intern, and everything considered, I had been a diligent worker and avoided taking shortcuts. Of course, not much would change if I became a regular employee. I'd qualify for national insurance and a slight increase in wages, but I'd also be expected to work overtime without complaining, so it wouldn't all be good news. Nor had I ever considered the academy as my final destination. Perhaps if I was doing content development at HQ. But a lowly regular employee at a small academy sounded like one compromise after another. Even so . . . What if I *was* offered a regular position? What should I say?

"Let's hire another intern."

This comment of Dept. Head Kim's threw all my vain worries out the window.

"And Jihye, you can write the job posting."

So, in the end, I had been worrying for nothing. In fact, the only thing that came of it was more work for me.

I posted a short ad on a few job sites. Hiring intern. Office clerk. Hourly pay, negotiable. Easy transfers to HQ. Of course, we wrote these last two lines out of "courtesy," like the way strangers make tentative lunch plans when both people know full well it will never happen. Dept. Head Kim and Team Leader Yu made a small wager over how many people would apply for the spot. When I was hired, the odds were fifty-seven to one. But beating out fifty-six applicants just to spend all day copying documents and stacking chairs was nothing to be proud about. They pestered me to make a bet too. "I doubt there'll be more than sixty applicants," I said. They scolded me for belittling our academy.

After the weeklong application period, we had a pool of eighty-four applicants. Team Leader won the bet, as she guessed eighty people would apply, and was more than happy to collect 10,000 won from me.

But on the day of the interview, Dept. Head Kim conveniently was out of the office. And because there was no way Director Park or Deputy Dept. Head Yun were going to sit in on interviews, it looked like Team Leader Yu was going to have to conduct all the interviews by herself.

"It looks like we lack commitment. We're DM, for God's sake. This isn't some part-time job at a coffee shop. We can't just have one interviewer in the room like this."

Team Leader Yu griped out loud to herself for a while before begrudgingly turning to me and asking me if I would join her in the interview room. There was a short pause before I agreed. Such was the dynamic between her and me. She proposed things, and I had to nod in agreement.

The overly solemn and dignified manner in which the interview was conducted didn't match the nature of the work that the intern would end up doing. Almost all the chairs and desks had been cleared out of the meeting room, leaving a large chasm between the interviewers and the interviewee. I spun a ballpoint pen on my fingers as I sat next to Team Leader Yu in the makeshift interview room.

"I'll handle everything. All you need to do is sit there with an arrogant look on your face."

Team Leader Yu leaned back in her chair with her arms crossed. Every so often, she would yawn without covering her mouth, and whenever she did this, her stale breath would waft all the way to where I was sitting. I pulled my shoulders back and straightened my back. Not feeling quite arrogant enough, I tried crossing my legs, which seemed to do the trick.

So this is what it feels like.

Sitting in this chair, I had the authority to cross my arms and legs. I could even interrupt the person to take a phone call if I wanted.

27

Interviewees assumed that I was a person of importance because I sat in this seat. Even if this was just an insignificantly small academy, my sitting here meant their fate was in my hands. But who was I kidding? I was only put in this chair as a stage prop to increase the head count. It could have been anyone. Hell, a lifelike mannequin might have done the trick.

As Team Leader Yu continued to curse Dept. Head Kim for ditching her, I sat and waited for the interviewees just as she instructed me to: with a look of arrogance.

The interviewees came from a diverse range of backgrounds. Most were students, either currently enrolled, coming back to school from the military, or taking time off from their studies. But there was also an aspiring webtoon writer, a professional bodyguard, and an actor looking to work two jobs. Each looked desperate in their own way, and each wore a uniquely jaded look on their face. And they all shared the same dark shadows beneath their eyes, as if collectively presenting the symptoms of having lived too long outside mainstream society. The uniformity of their appearances, which were too similar to be mere coincidence, shocked me and made me think: Do I look like that? Had there been a mirror in the room, I would have checked. We blasted through thirty-two interviews before it was time for lunch.

"Why are there so many people like this in the world? You know, the 'artistic unemployed.'"

The "artistic unemployed" was one of Team Leader Yu's favorite phrases. She said she was doing them a favor by referring to them as this instead of their official name: deadbeats. Indeed, Team Leader Yu always complained about how there were too many people in society wanting to do things like create music, literature, art, and film, and would bemoan how the artistic unemployed were "gnawing away at the foundations of society." Contrary to common knowledge, culture and academics were ultimately commodities to be bought and sold. The converse statement to this was that culture wasn't culture if it didn't make money. Of course, it wasn't only Team Leader Yu who thought like this, but nevertheless, it was a worldview that made me uncomfortable. When she suggested jjajangmyeon for lunch, I shook my head.

"I'm going out—my friend came to have lunch with me."

"Oh, you mean Mr. Jeong-jin? You should bring him to the office sometime. Tell him he can get an employee discount. But more importantly, shouldn't you guys make it official already?"

I left her with a lukewarm smile in lieu of an answer and exited the office.

* * *

I bought a banana, instant kimbap, and a carton of strawberry milk at the local convenience store. I swung the plastic bag to and fro as I trudged through the network of back alleys. When the old apartment building entered my field of view, I slowed my steps. I then let out a sigh long enough to expel the last molecule of oxygen from my lungs.

This apartment was an old complex that had somehow escaped untouched by the hurricane of redevelopment that once swept through the neighborhood. Its residents might feel differently, but I liked walking through this quaint and forlorn apartment complex weathered by the passage of time. There was a small trail behind the buildings that led to an open field. Wrapping around the field like a Greek amphitheatre was a half circle of stone steps. It would be a great place for concerts and plays, but judging from all the weeds, it seemed residents thought of it as nothing more than a useless empty lot.

I sat on the steps and took a sip of strawberry milk. This was where I usually came whenever I told people that Mr. Jeong-jin was coming to visit me at work. I had invented Jeong-jin as a lifeline from the stifling existence that was life in the city. Eating lunch with the same people day in and day out made it hard to breathe. Every day, it was the same script: "What do y'all want to eat? I'm fine with anything. How about pork cutlet? Sounds good. Should we all eat jjajangmyeon? Sure, why not." And then there was the tradition of the youngest making sure everyone had napkins and silverware and that no one's glass was ever empty. Of course, I put up with it because I knew that every company was like this. But even so, even so . . . sometimes, I just needed an escape.

So one day, I lied and said I was having lunch with a friend. After a few times of using this excuse, people started inquiring about this friend's gender, and once they knew he was a male, they wanted to know his name and age. And thus, Mr. Jeong-jin was born. Giving my imaginary friend a name that was a compound of jeongmal and jinjja, two words that both meant "real," was an inside joke that only I knew the punch line to. After a few times of being caught off guard by questions about Jeong-jin, Team Leader Yu concluded that he must like me and that we were in that initial stage of coquetry. It was too much trouble to fight her conjecturing, but I knew that at the rate things were going, I would end up marrying Jeong-jin if something didn't change. In other words, I had to break up with him before our relationship got too serious. I let out a smirk in disbelief thinking about how what had started as a simple white lie was now pushing me into a double life against my will. All I wanted was to eat lunch in peace, and now here I was, flirting, dating, and engaged-to-be-engaged to a man who didn't even exist.

"I'm so sorry, Mr. Jeong-jin. How could I have known things would turn out this way?"

As I whispered this to myself, real regret washed over me. But whom was my regret directed toward? Perhaps someone I wish I had? Someone I could lean against whenever I needed him? Someone just like Mr. Jeong-jin?

I munched on the banana and kimbap. Originally, I didn't have any intention of getting food, but I needed something in my stomach if I wanted to prevent its grumbling from interrupting the interviews. For dessert, I inhaled the fresh air. I then opened my mouth as wide as I could and let out a long, low yell. This was my secret for getting rid of all the toxins and lactic acid inside my body. Sometimes I accidentally ran into someone just as I was yodeling, but it was worth the embarrassment.

Weighing on my mind was the way I'd been sitting in that room with my mouth shut like a third wheel. Even if my presence was all for show, I might as well try to exercise my small amount of authority while I still had it. "Where do you see yourself in ten years?" This was the question I would ask them when I had the chance. I doubted anyone would give the correct answer: "Not here. God, I hope not. No, I'm just passing through. Don't think I want to work here until I'm old and crusty." If, however, someone did answer this way, and if I was actually in a position of power, I'd immediately offer them a job, plus incentives.

I daydreamed like this as I returned to the office. The door to the interview room was wide open, and I could hear Team Leader Yu grumbling again. "I told you there wouldn't be any promising candidates." I opened the door to find Dept. Head Kim sitting in the room and listening to Team Leader Yu. He said he'd be late, but he came back earlier than I'd expected.

"Oh, Jihye. Thank you. Now that Dept. Head Kim is here, you can go."

Team Leader Yu said this as she flipped through a stack of papers. I gave a slight bow of the head and left. From behind me came Team Leader Yu's voice telling me to copy lecture materials with the rest of my time.

And thus, I went back to my post feeding paper into an old copy machine. What was the extent of my role at this company? Glorified printer ink? Or perhaps I was just a spare bolt, replaceable and always getting screwed.

The shrill voice of a woman caused me to lift my head. From her detail-oriented and studious appearance, I could tell she was a student at a women's college. Eyes like a rabbit, she asked politely where the interview room was. I pointed to the meeting room without saying anything. Her hurried steps as she made her way in that direction were one gear short of a skip. I sifted through my memory of the resumes I'd seen earlier until I found hers. She was perfect, flawless. But being too perfect was a disadvantage, so she probably wouldn't make the cut.

Anyway, it was Friday. After coasting through the day, I bought myself several cans of discounted beer at the supermarket and made my way home: a cozy, clean room on the fifth floor of a small five-story apartment building—or at least, that's where my parents back in Wonju thought I lived. And back in college, that was exactly the type of apartment I had. But with time, as if to symbolize my trajectory in life, a fifth-floor apartment turned into a fourth-floor apartment, and then a third-floor apartment, and so on and so forth until I was living in a semi-basement room, the kind whose windows peeked up over the asphalt. If there was one upside, it was that I wasn't all the way underground or living in one of those goshiwon micro apartments. My parents were too busy tending to their strawberry farm to come up to Seoul very often. But never say never, so sometimes I would imagine what I would do if they suddenly showed up at my door. Thankfully, my fears had yet to become a reality.

I opened a can of beer and turned on the TV to watch some variety shows. On the screen was a bit of slapstick comedy as celebrities competed to see who could do the most pull-ups. I sipped on my beer as I observed their acting cute for the camera. It crossed my mind that in eight months, my lease would be up, and that the landlord had sworn to raise rent.

Put another way, I had just eight months to fix my life, to find answers. With a swig of beer, I tried to wash down the anxiety working its way up my esophagus. The celebrity on TV was telling a tear-filled story about how his business had failed and how his wife was always nagging him about it. But I had a feeling that the view from his window was of the ever-brightening city lights of downtown Seoul. I knew for a fact that this was what people who lived in high-up places would see. But I guess the view from everyone's window is slightly different.

I picked up my phone to check the time when I accidentally caught my reflection in the black LCD screen. I smiled back at myself, face flushed and eyes drowsy. They say smiling makes the brain dance. The physical act of smiling, even when you're not happy, literally causes your brain to produce dopamine and other feel-good hormones. The private life of this celebrity whom I've never met made me smile. Now that I was grabbing at my stomach and laughing, I could last a little bit longer, at least one more day.

4

MINIMAL WORKER

The symptoms of Mondayitis are vast and varied. In my case, puffy eyes are what signal the beginning of the week. Even if I haven't been drinking the night before, my lids are always swollen shut on Monday mornings.

I threw on a pair of glasses and left the house. Glasses cover many things. Exhaustion, irritability, tears—all of these were more or less equalized with a single pair of thick-rimmed glasses.

Despite my rush to get out the door, I was still four minutes late for work. As soon as I got out of the elevator, a booming voice from inside the office hit my ears. I gently pushed the door ajar and looked inside to see the back of a man who was one head taller than everyone else in the room. The man's unfamiliar husky voice broke through the hum of familiar chatter like a timpani.

"Oh, Jihye. You're here."

Team Leader Yu's voice was unusually sweet. It was so soft, even songlike, a composer might have labeled it cantabile. Tardiness usually warranted a long scolding, but she didn't seem bothered by my being late.

"Oh right, let me introduce you. This is our new intern."

The man turned around and gave me a polite bow of the head.

"Pleased to meet you. My name's Lee Gyuok."

Because he was large and wearing a thick, pilling fleece jacket, I thought we'd accidentally hired a talking polar bear. I bowed back. But when I realized this brought my face closer to his, I bowed even further to hide my puffy eyes, and before I knew it, my head was as low as my belly button.

"Oh, you don't have to bow that deeply to me."

Polar Bear's witty response made Team Leader Yu laugh. Didn't she know laughing like that only made me more embarrassed?

"Come to think of it, you two are the same age. That'll make working together much more comfortable. And seeing you standing together like this, I feel reassured in my choice."

Team Leader Yu said this as if she were admiring the new figurine she'd just added to her collection.

"Follow me," I said to Polar Bear. Team Leader Yu had instructed me to show him around, but there wasn't much to see. As we made one lap around the building, I explained to him how to buy office supplies and the rules for issuing refunds. After quickly pointing out the watercooler and vending machine, I showed each classroom to him by quickly opening and closing their doors. And then for the pièce de résistance: the copy machine. I took pride in explaining to him my philosophy behind replicating educational materials, but Polar Bear just gave me a perfunctory nod, as if he already knew everything that I was telling him. Last of all, I told him the "perks" of working at Diamant Academy.

"Interns are allowed to take one course free of charge every semester. Take a look through the course catalog and tell me what looks interesting to you."

"Hm, I'll have to think about that. What about you? What are you taking?" His voice was kind.

"I don't take any classes. I don't have time, and nothing really looks interesting to me."

"I see. Well, I look forward to working together. Oh, that reminds me. What's your name again?"

"Kim Jihye."

"Well, nice to meet you, Kim Jihye. That's a pretty name. Shall we shake?"

The corner of my mouth twitched as a smirk attempted to form on my lips. Come to think of it, this might have been the first time someone ever said my name was pretty. The handshake caught me off guard as well. I couldn't remember the last time I'd shaken someone's hand for work. In fact, I couldn't remember ever greeting someone with anything other than a formal bow. For the first time since meeting him, I raised my head to get a good look at this Lee Gyuok. The look in his eyes was good-natured. *That face . . . I swear I've seen it before. But where?* As I searched my memory, he held out his hand. It was in that moment that I saw it. The star-shaped tattoo on the back of his hand. This was the man I'd seen at the café! The one who shamed Professor Park in public, who sat next to me on the subway solving crossword puzzles. Here he was, now shaven and wearing contacts, offering to shake my hand.

* * *

I couldn't deny that work had become easier after Gyuok's arrival. He was strong enough to lift watercooler bottles with one hand and jumped to his feet to help Team Leader Yu whenever she was about to do something. He was quick on the uptake and courteous, qualities that all the seniors in the company liked. He put everyone in a good mood, so much so that even Team Leader Yu became less prickly. Amiable, well-mannered, and proactive. Perhaps it was because he was a new employee? But if that was the case, there'd be something forced about it. But his behavior was too natural for this to be a case of youthful eagerness.

And there was something else that I found odd. While he was always kind and friendly with everyone, sometimes he seemed detached, as though surrounded by a thin and transparent yet impenetrable veil. Was the way he presented himself really how he felt? He was full of energy, always made eye contact with whomever he was talking to, and had a broad smile that few would question as insincere. And yet, he avoided groups and had a curious habit of inconspicuously diverting any questions about his personal life. These were behaviors that you would miss if you weren't paying close attention. Indeed, if it weren't for that incident with Professor Park at the café, I would have missed them too.

Gyuok's resume, which I pulled up out of curiosity, was unassuming. A BA in philosophy from J University and no real work experience to speak of. I let out a sigh. Majoring in philosophy at a college that was only one notch better than a provincial university was as good as an early bird reservation for being unemployed out of college.

"Jihye, you really think resumes get people jobs here?" This was Team Leader Yu's response when I asked why she hired Gyuok. "I cut everyone with stacked resumes who vowed to devote themselves to the company because it was obvious that they were lying. I prefer people who make good first impressions."

I could see Team Leader Yu's reflection in the mirror. I'd always thought it amazing how Team Leader Yu could carry an entire conversation by herself as she noisily picked food from her teeth with a strand of floss. *Tack-tack-tack.*

"I hope you're not asking because you're interested. I mean, he's got a nice personality, and not half bad looking if you look hard enough, but as your superior, and as a fellow woman, I have to advise against it, Jihye. Dating is an investment. Meet someone who will improve your life."

Hearing this, I hawked a wad of toothpaste into the sink. She might have had a point, but I didn't feel comfortable treating human relationships like the stock exchange.

"And Jihye, you should take more care of your appearance. At your age, everyone should be complimenting you on your looks. I'm not saying you look bad or dress poorly. Don't take it that way. I just find it a shame that you don't dress up more or put on makeup. Later, when you're old and look back on your life, you'll regret having wasted your youth."

My pulse quickened as I momentarily became filled with anger, but when I looked at my reflection in the mirror, I found myself agreeing with her. Disheveled hair and a pair of red thick-rimmed glasses that had an annoying propensity to slide down to the tip of my nose. Pale, dry skin and lifeless eyes. Even I could see that this wasn't the face of a promising youth. Blinking at me from the glass was a woman whose facial expression was so drained it looked like it belonged to someone who'd just crawled out of a coffin.

Out in the hallway, Gyuok was on his knees wiping the power cord to the watercooler.

"You've gotta dust these places off regularly. It's the only way an office feels loved."

Sometimes, Gyuok volunteered himself to do pointless tasks that no one asked him to do. He gave me a big smile.

"Don't electrocute yourself," I said without smiling back at him and continued on my way. It wasn't that I was actually concerned for his safety, but rather that I didn't want him to die needlessly doing a job that no one had asked him to do.

One day, I asked Gyuok why he was such an overachiever, and he told me that he was only keeping the promise he'd made during the interview to "work hard" if he got the job. He also said that procrastinating on tasks around the office only created more work for others; wiping down surfaces was his way of helping out the cleaning ladies. I couldn't tell if he was unusually egalitarian or if he was just full of it, but two weeks into the job, and he still hadn't loosened up. In fact, everyone only had good things to say about him. Even Dept. Head Kim, who never had anything good to say about anyone, had praise to spare when it came to Gyuok.

I, on the other hand, did not welcome such foolish industriousness. People need to work in moderation. They needed to work according to what they were owed, according to the time and the money they were given. As irregular workers barely earning minimum wage, we needed to keep our efforts to a minimum and strike a delicate balance between saving face and practicality. There was a huge difference between a slacker who occasionally tries hard and a try-hard who occasionally slacks off. The former's efforts were praised, while the latter's screwups got criticized. You needed to straddle the line, sometimes pretending you couldn't do a job, and mess up intentionally once in a while to give your boss the chance to scold you and feel important. My ideal performance evaluation was as follows: "Barely does enough to get by. Clumsy, but shows flashes of competence." That was how you worked to protect yourself. Particularly when the work was tedious, unfulfilling, and paid like shit. Did thinking this way make me a jaded person? Or perhaps I just lacked dreams and aspirations.

Whenever I saw Gyuok failing to protect himself, I couldn't help but think about that incident at the coffee shop. I couldn't reconcile this obsequious Goody Two-shoes with that shouting man from the café. I considered the possibility that his working here might have something to do with Professor Park. But the professor wasn't teaching this semester; in fact, not long after the incident at the café, he left the country on an extended vacation. Because of this, there was no chance that he and Gyuok would have another coincidental collision at the academy.

If I were a regular employee, I wouldn't hesitate to tell Team Leader Yu all about the history between Gyuok and Professor Park. But as it was, I had no reason to. I was just an outsider looking in, the kind of person who had no business knowing other people's secrets, who had no obligation to improve workplace conditions. I wasn't going to stick my neck out for something that wouldn't benefit me.

CHAIRS

Late afternoon. It was another one of those days—tedious and cheerless, yellow sand and micro-dust blocking out the spring sun and turning the entire sky a foul orange color. Everyone was working off-site today—everyone except for Gyuok and me. Classes had ended for the day, leaving the academy in listless silence. We were both lost in our own worlds, and neither of us had spoken a word to each other in hours. But then a middle-aged man suddenly appeared through the front door, bringing Gyuok and me together again. The man said he was here to register for Professor Park's class.

"I'm sorry, but Professor Park isn't teaching this semester."

"What about in the fall?"

"We don't have the schedule yet. You'll have to wait until it's released."

The man nodded in disappointment before dragging his feet out of the office. His role had ended, but the name Professor Park lingered in the air like a stubborn echo. I glanced furtively toward

Gyuok. He was staring at his cell phone, a hand cupping his chin. With his mouth covered like that, I found it hard to tell what expression he was making. I cleared my throat, but he didn't seem to notice. If anyone was going to broach the subject, it would have to be me. But how?

"Still thinking about what class to take?" I asked, taking a shot in the dark.

"Yeah." Gyuok brushed off the question then put the ball back in my court. "Got any recommendations?"

I hadn't expected him to give me a chance to talk about Professor Park so easily. I licked my upper lip eagerly.

"I've got one in mind. Unfortunately the professor's not teaching this semester. It's a shame. Professor Park's class is our most popular course."

Hopefully, this was on the nose enough to elicit a reaction. Now it was time to observe. But to my surprise, not a muscle in his face so much as twitched.

"I see. I'm sure there'll be more opportunities in the future."

He then smiled at me, putting his whole face into it.

I'd read that polygraphs measure slight changes in electrical conductivity created by the perspiration we produce when nervous. But for some reason, I doubted Gyuok's fingertips were sweating as he made that cool expression. The smile he gave me really looked like he'd never met Professor Park before.

"Well, shall we go move chairs?" he asked. Even his timing for ending this conversation was perfect. Had he changed the subject just a second earlier, it might have sounded like he was avoiding this topic.

Chairs were invariably dispersed and misaligned after each

class, and it was our job to reorganize them. A dusty beam of sunlight was falling obliquely on the chairs. I narrowed my eyes and stalled. A strange yet familiar sensation washed over my brain. I forced myself to move, ridding my mind of the thought. But just as I started moving chairs, Gyuok's voice sounded from behind me.

"What was that?"

"Come again?"

"I'm just curious why you hesitated when we first entered the room."

His curiosity struck me as unusual. I'd never been asked a question like that, so trivial it made me wonder why he even bothered asking it.

"It's the light. I hate the sunlight at this time of day. When the light falls sideways like this, it means that the sun is beginning to set, and that you've wasted another day doing nothing. I've always hated twilight since I was a kid. Anyway! Let's get to work."

I clapped my hands together as I said "anyway" to make the end of my story less depressing. But in comparison to the large motion of my hands coming together, the sound they made was laughably quiet and airy.

Gyuok, however, just leaned against the wall motionless, his arms crossed. He stood there like that for a while before pointing at something with his finger.

"Come over here and take a look at this."

"Take a look at what?"

His finger was pointing toward the middle of the empty room. I stood next to him, put my back against the wall like a grade school student in time-out, and looked down the length of his arm with an expression of displeasure on my face. I still couldn't see it. It was just a messy post-lecture classroom, something I saw almost every day. Placid, like a school classroom once the children have gone home. I couldn't see what he was making such a big deal about.

"I'm looking but I don't see it."

Gyuok wiggled his finger to indicate he was pointing at the mess of chairs.

"Jihye, you move chairs several times a day. But what do you think when you look at them?"

"I don't know. Hurry up? Get to work?"

Gyuok nodded his head as he clicked his tongue, a reaction I found somewhat irksome and unnecessarily abstruse.

"You know, most people don't nod their head while clicking their tongue. Those two gestures usually mean the opposite thing."

Gyuok put his hand down and started walking toward the middle of the room.

"It means that I understand your answer but don't agree with it."

I batted my eyelids in annoyance. What was there to agree with? He'd asked me what I thought, and I told him.

"Well, on the surface, it's the obvious answer. It's your job, and those chairs *should* be moved."

"Yeah?"

"But let's look at it from a different perspective. What's the function of a chair?"

"Sitting."

"Right. You can't eat a chair. You sit on it. Anyone can sit here and listen to a lecture if they've paid their tuition. But what's that chair over there?"

He pointed to the teacher's chair at the front of the classroom. Unlike the foldable chairs for students, the teacher's chair was an expensive antique chair, complete with elaborate ornamentation. Each classroom had one chair like this.

"You have to be a lecturer to sit in that chair," I explained, remembering the one time I got to sit in that exact chair and pretend like I was an interviewee. "You either have to study for many years and become an expert in your field, or you need to be famous enough so that envious people want to learn from you. But so what?"

Gyuok stroked his chin. "It's not just the chairs in this room. There's something magical about all chairs. Imagine yourself sitting in that chair up there. Suddenly you're put under a spell. You're under the illusion that you have power, that you have authority. But if you sit in these chairs down here, you're put under a different spell. You think you're part of the powerless masses. You nod your head in agreement to whatever the person up there says. But they're just chairs. How come we forget that?"

When Gyuok finished, he turned and winked at me. Did he really think that spouting off a bunch of pseudo-philosophical bullshit made him cool?

I scoffed, accidentally betraying the fact that I wasn't impressed. I hadn't intended to offend him, but it seemed like my reaction embarrassed Gyuok, who withdrew his head into his shoulders as he shrugged.

"I guess I got carried away," he said. "Sorry." Gyuok didn't waste any more time and started moving the chairs by himself. I felt a little bad for being so mean to him.

"Actually, there is a course I want to take," Gyuok said as he paused.

"And what's that?"

"Ukulele for Beginners. Wanna take it together?"

"Ukulele?"

This was so unexpected it left me speechless. Of all the courses he could take, Beginning Ukulele was his choice? As one of only a handful of music courses on our catalog, it was something we only offered because we wanted to look like a well-balanced liberal arts academy. It wasn't a class for serious students. And if I was being totally honest, I thought that music appreciation was the only music education most people needed. Plus, if I were to learn to play an instrument, the ukulele would be toward the bottom of that list.

I'd told Gyuok that one of the benefits of working here was the free course interns were allowed to take advantage of once a semester. But technically, that was a lie. Every month, money was subtracted from our paychecks to fund this benefit, whether we signed up for a class or not. In some ways, it was the exact opposite of free. Because of this, some felt the need to take the class, a sort of sunk-cost fallacy for the exploited. But as for me, the only thing worse than wasting money was wasting time *and* money taking a class I was never interested in in the first place. Keep my money, but just don't take my time.

"The ukulele class costs ten thousand won more than the other courses and meets two less times. That means it's the most expensive class per hour."

"That's your reason for taking it? Seems a bit miserly to me."

"On the contrary. If they're going to force this benefit on us, we should be smart about it. If not, we let them take everything away from us and never get anything back in return. We're allowing injustice to prevail. And besides, it's the ukulele. Just imagine yourself going to Hawaii one day and playing the ukulele while doing the hula. Isn't that romantic?"

Gyuok laughed with his shoulders. He had a habit of always showing a row of white teeth when he laughed, even for the briefest of chuckles. Sometimes, his Adam's apple even moved back and forth with his shoulders. He looked so naïve, and I barely held myself back from telling him he could do it by himself.

But as we continued to fold chairs, I started to think he might be right. At first, I thought his argument was just the justification of a man trying to make the most out of money he'd already lost, but now that I thought about it, he had a point. If I didn't take this free ukulele class while I had the chance, not only would I be letting myself get exploited, but I'd also be forever cursed to live a life lacking in romance, unable to play the ukulele while dancing the hula in Hawaii. And that to me seemed like an unbearably depressing fate.

When we finished moving chairs, we stopped at the vending machine for a cup of instant coffee. Gyuok held his cup up to me for a toast. I stared at if for a moment before reluctantly holding mine up as well. The sound of two paper cups "clinking" felt somewhat anticlimactic. The hot liquid sloshed back and forth for a second.

"Cheers—"

"Cheers . . ."

I was still wary of him. But something had changed. Having toasted like this, it felt like we had become accomplices in a heist, a feeling that would soon become a reality.

* * *

Nine chairs were neatly arranged in a classroom. In attendance were Gyuok, me, three elementary school students, accompanied by two mothers, and two men, one in his fifties, the other in his thirties.

As was always the case just before the start of a class, the room was noisy with antsy anticipation as people waited for the instructor. I went up to the front of the classroom and informed them that the instructor was running ten minutes late. But twenty minutes later, he still hadn't arrived, and people were starting to give me sideways glances. I regretted revealing that I worked here.

"If I knew this would happen—" I whispered to Gyuok, "I would have made you deliver the bad news. Should we wait outside until he arrives?"

Before we could excuse ourselves, one of the students finally spoke up. It was the older gentleman sitting in front of us.

"How long are you going to make us wait? I hope you plan to hold class late. I want my money's worth."

Now sneaking out of the classroom would be impossible. It was at that very moment that the door opened and the instructor came into the classroom, beads of sweat rolling down his face. It was his first day on the job, and he'd arrived more than thirty minutes late. He apologized, explaining that he'd gotten stuck in traffic, but every time he opened his mouth, I could smell the stench of alcohol on his breath.

There was this hit K-drama ten years ago whose soundtrack was about as popular as the show itself. It just so happened that the ukulele player from the indie duo who wrote and performed the OST for that drama was none other than the instructor for our class. The combination of his ukulele and her vocals was beautiful and ephemeral, like they'd come straight out of a fairy tale. But when the vocalist got married and left the group, he lost all motivation to write music. Now on the cusp of middle age, he was a has-been artist still riding on the coattails of his own fifteen minutes of fame from over a decade ago. In fact, I'd reviewed his resume, which was barely propped up by that one-hit soundtrack, and I'd wager that the only source of income he had aside from this minor teaching gig were the measly royalty checks he occasionally received in the mail.

Hungover and in need of a shower, he'd prepared the same half-assed lesson plan that all lazy lecturers prepare for their first day of class: useless opening remarks and tedious self-introductions. Actually, one of the reasons I hadn't taken advantage of my "free" course until now was precisely because I didn't want to expose myself to the mandatory self-introductions that always happened on the first day of class. For some reason, self-introductions always made a mess of me. Even if people swore I did fine, that wasn't how I felt.

I've always wondered why people in group-learning environments need to introduce themselves. My worst memory of self-introductions was made last year while taking swimming lessons, just after I turned twenty-nine. Afraid they might make us introduce ourselves, I'd skipped the first four days of class, just to be extra safe. But I must have the worst luck, because as soon as I got into the water, the instructor said, "Well, now that we're all familiar with each other, why don't we introduce ourselves? Go around the circle and say your name, age, and occupation." To my surprise, I was the only one who looked nervous. "I'm nineteen, and I'm just starting college." "I'm twenty-two and I just finished my mandatory military service. I'm doing this to stay in shape." Surrounded by such young people with bright futures, there was absolutely no way I was going to admit that I was unemployed and entering my thirties. When it was finally my turn to talk, I reflexively lied, saying that I was twenty-five and had just started working at such-and-such company.

After that, we spent the remaining forty-five minutes of class hanging from the swimming pool wall, paddling like our lives depended on it, goggles and swim caps squeezing our skulls. When you really thought about it, there was no reason—not even a bad one—for people taking a swimming class together to know each other's ages or occupations. As I brought my head in and out of the water to gasp for oxygen, I wondered if I could maintain this lie for as long as it took me to become a good swimmer, this lie that I was a twenty-five-year-old employee at such-and-such company.

I got my answer soon enough. That day after taking my post-lesson shower, I was in the locker room putting on my clothes when someone came up to me and told me that their friend also worked at such-and-such company. "Oh, really?" I said, half naked and astounded at my bad luck. My only goal at that moment was getting out of there before she asked me for my business card. I frantically threw on my clothes—something that's unreasonably hard to do when your body is still moist—and was just about to leave when something fell onto the floor. It was the book I had accidently left in the locker. Plastered on the front cover like text on a flashy billboard were the words: GET HIRED NOW! BECOME AN EXPERT AT JOB INTERVIEWS! It was my first and last swimming lesson. And, just like that, I'd already broken my New Year's resolution of learning how to swim, all because of that damned self-introduction.

As I got lost in this dark memory, the three elementary school stu-dents were telling everyone what school they attended and the name of their teacher that year, as if "Mrs. Cho" meant anything to us. The rhythmic delivery of their introductions reminded me that children up to a certain age love to tell strangers all about themselves. The instructor was taking this chance to get settled in and wipe the sweat off his neck. The mothers also introduced themselves by telling us which child or children were theirs, instead of actually giving us their names, and as they did this, the teacher grinned, clasping his hands over the knees of his now-crossed legs as though pleased with himself about how receptive the class was to his lesson plan.

The mother with two children, one boy and one girl, was your typical social soccer mom and had no trouble talking about herself and her children for several minutes. She explained that she enrolled them in the class to cultivate their musical sensibility and educate them in the arts, adding that these days, not learning an instrument was a fast track to getting bullied at school. The second mother, whose son looked just like her, began in a quivering voice as she stroked her son's hair. Apparently, he had originally wanted to learn the guitar, but she was a bit concerned that the guitar would be too large for him, so she made him take up the ukulele, which had the added benefit of being considerably less expensive. When it came time to talk about herself, she said that she enrolled herself in the course with her son because she wanted to rediscover her purpose in life through music. She continued to tell us her whole life story, how her husband was always busy with work, how she'd devoted herself to raising their son, how once he was old enough to go to school, she began to wonder if she was wasting her life. Watching the instructor nod his head without ever breaking eye contact, I was beginning to feel like I'd stumbled into a group therapy session. Gyuok looked at me out of the corner of his eye before whispering to me.

"Know what you're going to say?"

"No. I hate self-introductions. I should never have signed up for this class."

"Hate it or not, I doubt you're going to make it out of here without giving one."

His tone was contrarian, as though trying to provoke me. Because the two gentlemen took their cue from the mothers, each giving long-winded confessions, by the time it was my turn, twenty minutes had already flown by. Everyone's head turned to me. I cracked opened my dry lips and began to recite what I'd gone over in my head.

"My name's Kim Jihye. I'm a part-time worker here at the academy. I want to take up the ukulele as a hobby."

I lied and said I was a part-time worker, instead of an intern, because I thought it would require less explanation. People were generally dismissive of adult part-time workers, but there was something about being an intern in your thirties that piqued people's interest, as though they couldn't understand why a failure wouldn't accept defeat. Silence filled the room. It looked like everyone thought I had something more to say.

"Nice to meet everyone."

"Good," the teacher said as he scratched his eyebrow, clearly thinking it wasn't "good."

But what did he have to be unhappy about? Could there be a more concise and to-the-point self-introduction as the one I'd just given? I knew he was thinking it fortunate that I hadn't gone first. Had I gone first, everyone after me would have followed suit and given equally short self-introductions. Gyuok quickly took the baton from me.

"Lee Gyuok. I work here just like Ms. Kim. I chose to take this class after learning I could take courses for free."

"For free?" The teacher asked this in disbelief.

Gyuok quickly explained that employees were allowed to take one class free of charge every semester. The way the teacher's eyes started tracing the corners of the ceiling gave me the impression that he was doing some mental math, trying to figure out how much he would need to subtract from his already meager paycheck.

"Of course, I was always interested in learning the ukulele. It sounds pretty good despite looking like a toy."

"Pretty good? I'll have you know that countless masterpieces have been written for the ukulele."

The teacher folded his arms in offense. Gyuok raised both hands in the air and waved them, as if to say he hadn't meant to insult the man's instrument.

"Oh, no. That's not what I meant."

"Perhaps we should start class?" It was the mother, the one who seemed like she was suffering from depression. "It's already been an hour."

Thanks to this arbitration, we all took out our instruments from their cases, finally. Gyuok and my instruments were borrowed from the academy. I examined the cute little instrument, a small wooden box with just four nylon strings. The teacher taught us the basics of the instrument: the name of each part, how to hold it, and what note each string was tuned to. All of us plucked the four strings with our thumbs as we learned the notes la, mi, do, sol. Telling us that we needed to memorize the open strings, he instructed us to repeat after him: LA MI DO SOL, SOL DO MI LA, AECG, GCEA. We all did what he told us to do; I was probably the only one who looked bored.

"Since this is the first class, I think we can stop here. Are there any questions?"

The teacher awkwardly rubbed his palms together. He'd been glancing up at the clock this entire time, and despite everything, it was still twenty minutes before class was scheduled to be over. The hand of the depressed woman's son shot up.

"Can you introduce yourself?" he said eagerly.

The teacher made a bad joke about how he didn't have a wife to introduce, a pun made possible because the words "yourself" and "wife" were homonyms. Not understanding the joke, the boy glanced at his mother, who knitted her brow disapprovingly. Seeing this, the teacher brought his fist up to his mouth and cleared his throat. Then he gave in, telling everyone his name, his ex-band, and his claim-to-fame, decade-old soundtrack. Sadly, it seemed like no one sitting in the room that day, except for me, had ever heard of his band nor their songs.

As soon as class ended, I immediately ran back to the office and checked my online shopping order. I was already too late. The ukulele I'd ordered for myself late last night had already shipped. Even though I was taking this class because of Gyuok, the true reason for this disaster was the movie *Breakfast at Tiffany's*, which I'd watched on cable television a couple nights prior. If only I hadn't seen that movie, I never would have let Gyuok convince me to take this "free" course. If only Audrey Hepburn hadn't looked so stunning on the windowsill with her hair in a towel and singing "Moon

River," I never would have daydreamed about singing to the moon from my own windowsill. Of course, I'd forgotten that the view from my room wasn't of the moon but of the shoes and cigarette butts. Only later did I learn that the instrument Audrey Hepburn had been playing wasn't a ukulele but a mini guitar. How could I think it was a good idea to spend three months with a bunch of strangers learning from a lazy instructor with an over-inflated ego? In what universe did that sound like a good time?

* * *

Peace to me was meeting three times a week to study for the TOEIC in a proper classroom setting. Fifty students paying quiet attention to the teacher's thorough explanations of the different question types—that was what I wanted. There was a wide range of ages in my TOEIC class, everyone from young college students to people with tired faces who looked to be at least in their midthirties. Posted in front of the academy was a slogan a bit too grandiose for an English academy: "Say hello to the new you and goodbye to your old self."

It had been quite some time since I started using half of my paycheck from one academy to pay for an English class at another. I'd be lying if I said I was studying hard. But attending a TOEIC academy was a form of insurance—insurance of the mind, a promise to myself that I wasn't going to settle, that I was preparing for the future, that I was better today than I was yesterday. And to my delight, there were never any uncomfortable incidents here. Even though we were all potential competitors, because we were too busy competing with ourselves, we never paid attention to one another. And most important, the teacher never made us do anything stupid, especially not making self-introductions. TOEIC prep courses were always strictly business, no tomfoolery here, ten times better and more useful than any ukulele class could ever be.

The score I receive on my TOEIC exam after sacrificing several weeks of my life to study was much worse that it should have been, especially considering how expensive the tuition was. My score was well above average, of course, but the fifty points that I'd hoped to increase my score by never materialized. And when I realized that saving the money to buy fresh apples to make my cheeks rosier would be a better investment for my future, I decided to stop my monthly payments.

Today was my last day of TOEIC class, and so naturally I was focusing extra hard. I felt grateful that no one would notice when I failed to show up for class in a few days, after months of perfect attendance. Funnily enough, my reason for continuing to take the ukulele class despite my displeasure with it was for exactly the opposite reason: the shame that everyone would notice when I went missing.

6

COUP, BREAK, OR PRANK?

A fter class, when the instructor and the mothers and their children were gone, the man in his fifties suggested that the "adults" go out for drinks. Gyuok hesitated for a moment before saying he'd join them. He always avoided company dinners, but it seemed that he didn't mind going out for drinks with strangers. The other man in the class, a skinny fellow in his thirties, also expressed interest. Realizing this might be more of a guys' night out, I fell back on one of my usual excuses.

"Can't. Meeting up with a friend."

"Who? A boyfriend perhaps? Or maybe an ex?"

"I wish. A future boyfriend would be even better."

I gulped in embarrassment, realizing I'd just unintentionally confessed my relationship status, all past, present, and future.

"Well, if you get bored, you're free to join us whenever."

As I left, I could feel Gyuok's gaze following me.

It was past six and the sun was hanging low in the sky. But despite the evening chill, the air still felt alive with the afternoon's energy. I didn't feel hungry, so I decided to go to the movies. No matter how tight I was on money, I had a rule of going to a movie or an art exhibition at least once a month. Such artsy luxury was in part out of respect for myself, a kind of minimum investment toward my dream of one day becoming a person for whom culture was a career.

I was torn between two options. The first was a drama about a government worker who fights back after getting laid off, and the second was a mindless action film—superhuman heroes and interstellar bad guys. The first movie had two things going for it. Not only did it star one of my favorite actors, but I also seemed to recall that it had good reviews from critics. But in the end, I chose the second movie. After a long day at work, the last thing I wanted to do was think. I bought the small caramel popcorn and Coke special at the concession stand and waded through a mire of strangers' knees to my seat in the middle of the theatre. The movie was exciting enough. Crunching on my popcorn, I lost myself in sensory overload as gravity-defying action and dubious plot points flashed before my eyes.

At one point, I became curious about the faces of the other audience members and turned around to find people mesmerized by the film, chewing on popcorn and tearing off pieces of dried squid. When I turned back toward the screen, reality faded from me. For those two-plus hours it took the hero to save the universe and give the villain his comeuppance, I was completely and totally removed from the real world.

As the credits began to roll, I was ejected from the movie theatres by a wave of people. Walking through the streets, a selleongtang restaurant caught my eye just as I was starting to feel hungry. There was a long line of people waiting outside the restaurant, and I could hear the sound of various foreign tongues. Because I was alone and only needed a table for one, I skipped in front of the couples and families waiting for their numbers to be called. Before I knew it, a steaming bowl of soup was placed in front of me. But my heart didn't feel any warmer, even after putting all that hot liquid in my stomach. I looked at the time. Just past nine. A heavy sigh escaped my lips. I went into a convenience store to buy a can of beer, but just before pulling it out of the refrigerator, I paused. I took out my cell phone and started composing a text message. It took several attempts before the text sounded effortless and cool.

—Just said goodbye to my friend. Still hanging out?

I got a reply immediately. It was just four words, but a feeling of welcomeness spread through my chest.

—Of course! Hurry up!

The address he sent me was for a small underground bar, the kind with bookshelves full of vintage LPs. It was mostly empty by the time I arrived, so it took me no time to identify a table with three men. Gyuok's hand shot up as soon as he saw me. I took a bottle of beer out of the fridge and sat down to join the conversation, which was currently being led by the younger skinny man, whose sunken cheeks and high cheekbones cast deep shadows across his face. Already drunk, he was rocking back and forth in his chair while relating a story that was either something that he'd experienced personally or a rumor he'd heard about some celebrity,

I couldn't tell which. He was tall, like an old bamboo stalk, and I'd guess he was about the same weight as me, if not a bit lighter. Digging through my memory, I recalled that during class he'd introduced himself as a screenwriter. He had an unusual name. What was it again? I considered whether it would be impolite to ask if any of his screenplays had been made into movies. Thankfully, he answered both of my questions without my having to ask them.

"My dream is to see my name on the big screen. Screenplay by Kohmu Ingan. And people will scratch their heads saying, 'Rubberman?' It's a trend in the pop music scene for songwriters to use stage names like Shinsadong Tiger or Duble Sidekick. The film industry hasn't caught on yet. My real name, Koh Muin, is kind of boring. The other option is Koh Mushin, but that sounds like Rubber Shoe. So, I want to go by the name Kohmu Ingan—Rubberman."

That's what his name was. Koh Muin, not Rubber Shoe.

"This is a bit of a tangent, but there's this movie called *The Last Rubber Man*, I think it was originally titled *Bad Taste* in English. It's Peter Jackson's magnum opus. Of course he's most well-known for *Lord of the Rings* and *The Hobbit*, but I think his best work is *The Last Rubber Man*. Back then, at least, he was a serious artist who never compromised."

If I remembered correctly, Peter Jackson also directed *King Kong*. I realized Muin was the type to turn his nose up at famous Hollywood directors. He probably thought second-rate experimental films from no-name directors were works of art. Sour grapes, so to speak. Jealous because he couldn't have what they had.

Muin explained that he was taking a break from working right now—he was ambiguous as to the reason why—and that the main characters of the screenplay he'd been writing before taking a break played the ukulele. That was why he wanted to learn ukulele. But he was disappointed by the scale of the instrument now that he'd had a chance to play it himself, and grumbled to himself about how he thought he might need to rework the story.

"But that's amazing!" said the older portly man who'd mentioned during his self-introduction that he had a daughter in junior high school. "You're a writer! Not just anyone can write, you know. Right now, you gotta watch what you say wherever you go. Everyone's so obsessed with pointing out mistakes. Harmless posts on the internet will get you droves of comments correcting your grammar. Hell, even TV shows these days are including captions to correct for poor grammar. If you write *neomu* people will correct you and say its *aju*. But there's a huge difference between the two, isn't there? It's like the English *very* and *a lot*. I can't explain it, but there's truly a huge difference."

He seemed like the type to never stop talking once he got started. I wanted to point out that both were acceptable depending on the context but couldn't bring myself to do so.

"Awhile back, I was asked to write a short memoir of my childhood for my college reunion. So, I opened the word processor and started writing. *When I was in primary school . . .* That's what we called it back in the day, a remnant from the last years of Japanese colonial rule. But as soon as I typed the words, it automatically corrected it to *When I was in elementary school.* I tried to change it back, but the damned machine kept fighting me. I eventually had to give up. Fuck, I never went to *elementary* school, I tell you!"

"I've had similar experiences," I said, inserting myself into the conversation. "Autocorrect used to make all kinds of mistakes. I once typed Jacques Derrida, and it changed it automatically to Jacket Delivery."

My remark made Muin and the other man wrinkle their fore-heads.

"Who's Jacket Delivery?"

"No. Jacques Derrida. The French philosopher? Well techni-cally he was born in Algeria."

The furrows on their brows got even deeper. I regretted trying to join the conversation.

"I completely agree with you, though." I raised my hand as I said this as if to make a pledge. "*Neomu* can't be always substituted with *aju*."

The men all sucked air through tight lips, as though I were a lost cause.

"You said during class that your daughter was in junior high, right? I bet she's adorable."

The man's face lit up as soon as I mentioned his daughter. I hadn't expected my desperate attempt to change the subject to be such a success. The man took out his phone and flipped through the pictures for a while before showing me one of his daughter. Glow-ing on the screen was a coy girl whose well-contoured face didn't share much in common with her scruffy-looking father. He'd never looked so happy as when showing off that picture of his daughter.

"She's all I got. I changed her diapers. I gave her baths. But if I mention that now, she gets all huffy and runs to her room. I had to because her mother was busy. There's never been a father and daughter who were as close as me and her. At least until she hit damned puberty, that is. She was perfectly fine until one day she started slamming her bedroom door at the slightest provocation. And then one day, she stops studying. Says she wants to become a *K-pop* star or something. I tried to be supportive, but then one day,

I lost my cool. Everything went to hell after that. I want to make it up to her somehow. That's why I'm learning an instrument. I want her to know that I understand her."

He hadn't mentioned any of this during his self-introduction. We also learned that his wife had gone abroad to become a dancer, and that he was raising his daughter by himself.

"By the way, I don't know if you'll remember, but my name's Nam Eun. My legal name is Nam Eunju, but it's such a girly name. I usually tell people just to call me Nam Eun. Maybe that's why my wife left me to go to Turkey to become a belly dancer. And now that my daughter's getting too old for her dad, I guess I'm all alone now."

The man let out a wry laugh before asking me my name. Indeed, it was rare for people to remember names they'd heard only once. Yet again, I was reminded of the uselessness of self-introductions.

"Kim Jihye."

"Right, right. Ms. Jihye. Ms. Wise!"

A typical dad joke, but one I'd surprisingly never heard before. Because my name sounded like the word for "wise," it was low-hanging fruit for any adult male. I asked him to call me Sophia instead (my Christian name), but he ignored my wishes and continued to refer to me as Ms. Wise.

Gyuok barely said anything. He sat next to me and would say just the right amount to avoid looking like a party pooper, occasionally pouring people more alcohol if their glasses were empty and asking short clarifying questions. As one story morphed into another, we all began to relax, and before long, even I was enjoying myself and cracking witty jokes. Thinking it was time to get up, I tried lifting my body, which somehow had wound up sprawled on the couch, but the alcohol had already seeped into every corner of my body, and before long, I was drifting off into a blissful sleep.

* * *

We've all had that experience of suddenly being jolted awake at a party after having one too many drinks. The thing that spurred me out of my stupor was the word "coup d'état." It wasn't the kind of word you often heard in jazz bars in Seoul, at least, not these days. Coup d'état. Perhaps I was hearing things. But I was sure that's what I heard. I cracked open my eyes and rustled my body to pretend like I hadn't fallen asleep. Gyuok was leading the conversation.

"What we need is a coup. Not a coup you can see with your eyes but a coup of the mind."

There was a glint in his eyes as he leaned forward toward those listening to him. The others were quiet and had serious looks on their faces.

"Let's go back to what we were talking about earlier. If you had gotten that contract for your screenplay like you wanted, Muin, you wouldn't be here spreading celebrity gossip. Right? You'd be too busy writing your next masterpiece. And you too, Mr. Nam. I doubt you'd have time to spare from your busy schedule to come here and learn the ukulele. Even if we'd met by chance, we wouldn't be sitting here late into the night drinking together and talking about what could have been. Really, ask yourselves. Why *are* we drinking late into the night together and talking about what could have been? We were all wronged at some point. That's why."

It seemed like I'd missed a lot. I listened in, trying to glean from context everything that I'd missed. Mr. Nam, it seemed, had been unfairly forced to close his restaurant business for some reason.

The studio that adapted Muin's screenplay into a movie completely changed the story without his permission. The shock from it made him stop working for several months.

"The reason you can't write isn't simply a matter of blank-page syndrome," Gyuok said. "You're afraid of the system."

"Blank what?" Mr. Nam asked.

"You know, writer's block?" Muin answered. "But you're right. When I see that flashing cursor on my screen, my body freezes. I'm afraid someone will change whatever I end up putting down on paper. I was happy to write for free. With every page I wrote, it felt like I was discovering myself. But after that incident, I couldn't write a single word. The only reason I kept going was because I knew that I was doing what I loved. How did it come to this?"

"That's because the powerful minority are always confident." Gyuok was speaking slowly. "And the weak majority think that they can't change anything."

"So what do you mean by a coup? You want us to fight against the rich? Or should we find like-minded people and protest? I'm not even sure who I'm fighting against. Let's say, hypothetically, we did take some sort of action. What would change? You know what the powerful minority has that we don't? Money. In the end, it's all about money. It's not just South Korea. The whole world dances to the song of capitalism. Not even God can change it."

Gyuok lifted his eyes and looked Mr. Nam in the eyes. "The world will never get better, not if you keep thinking like that. Injustice shouldn't be whispered about. We need to act. That's what I mean by coup. Believing that we can right one small wrong, even if we can't change the world—that's the kind of coup I'm talking about. A moral coup."

"Hey—"

As soon as I opened my mouth, the room went quiet, like someone splashing cold water onto a fire.

"This is unexpected coming from a hardworking employee like you, Gyuok. Let's say we do stick it to one of the bigwigs at work. Then what? We'll be on their bad side and have to deal with their constant attempts to make life even more miserable for us."

I took a gulp of the beer I had remaining in my bottle, so lukewarm and flat, it almost tasted like barley tea.

"Also, taking this ukulele class, if you really think about it, is actually helping Dept. Head Kim. Before you start talking about coups, you first need to stop helping Dept. Head Kim. You need to break him. Anyway, coup or not, as long as I don't have to listen to him burping in the office anymore, I'll consider it a victory."

"Aha—" Gyuok laughed as though he knew exactly why I brought up Dept. Head Kim.

The mere mention of Dept. Head Kim's name was enough to put a frown on anyone's face. In fact, the only way I'd made it this long at the academy was because I did my best to stay as far away from him as possible. On the days I was unfortunate enough to sit across from him at lunch, I had to eat my meal while watching him pick his teeth with his fingers and eat whatever he found in there. He also had this horrible habit of giving expression to all the biochemical reactions happening inside his body. He burped, farted, and scratched his head without giving a damn about where the discharge from his body landed.

One time when I was talking one-on-one with him, he burped in my face, giving me a taste of the microbiome developing inside his mouth. I immediately felt nauseated and had to excuse myself and run to the bathroom. It was Team Leader Yu who patted my back as I leaned over the toilet. "Just hold in there a bit longer. It could be worse. Just be thankful it's gas and not another state of matter." I couldn't tell if she was being serious or whether she was just trying to make light of a bad situation. Either way, it was the first time she'd ever expressed sympathy. When I told this story to the others, Muin and Mr. Nam laughed so hard they had to grab their stomachs.

"You know, I'm a middle-aged man, too, so I understand. Aren't you being a little mean, though?" Mr. Nam said as he dabbed the tears in his eyes. "He probably lacks confidence. Maybe his flatulence is how he copes."

"I agree. It's funny but also a bit mean-spirited to hate someone over something like that." Muin seemed to be trying to display empathy for my boss, as though he felt guilty for laughing so hard. "I know it's a bit gross, but it's just an issue of etiquette. It doesn't make him a bad person."

"But it's not just the gas. Dept. Head Kim stinks up the whole system," I said.

If someone asked me what the worst part of working at the academy was, my initial reaction would be to say Team Leader Yu. After all, it didn't get much worse than a boss who liked to nag and give her employees more work just before going home. But, if you thought about it, at least she was consistent. She believed in everything she stood for. She was too honest to scheme like other bosses did. So even though I disliked the way she did things, I didn't hate her for it.

The same couldn't be said for Dept. Head Kim, the real villain of the office. His job was to sit at the neck of the company and control blood flow to and from the brain. As long as he remained in the company, the opinions of the people at the bottom would never make their way to the top. And because of that, our academy was much less democratic than it could be.

In fact, it was Dept. Head Kim who designed the intern system at the academy. Of course, internships in themselves weren't a horrible concept. A system that gave water to young, promising sprouts to see how well they did before hiring them as regular employees was a good way to promote development in the company and encourage productivity. The problem was that the system wasn't being used the way it was supposed to be.

Originally, after the three-month internship was up, the company was supposed to decide whether an intern's performance was good enough to warrant their being hired as a regular employee. But the academy had yet to promote any of its interns to regular positions. And all interns who weren't promoted had to leave the company. Once the old intern was gone, the company would start receiving new intern applications to fill the void, and the cycle would repeat. In this sense, you could say that my situation was unprecedented. I'd been working here for over nine months, but I still hadn't been hired as a regular employee. I was an "extended intern," whatever that meant. It was also Dept. Head Kim's idea to take a set amount from intern paychecks every month to pay for the "free" courses. This was just one of the many reasons I considered myself more of a part-time worker than a bona fide intern.

One time, in response to Team Leader Yu recommending me for a regular position, Dept. Head Kim said, as he cleaned the dirt from beneath his fingernails, "People apply to this position fully aware they won't be hired at the end of the internship. Surely Miss Jihye knows that." Indeed, as someone who had been exiled from headquarters to toil away the rest of his career at the academy (at least according to the rumors I'd heard), Dept. Head Kim didn't think much of the academy as a career destination.

Based on his reaction, Gyuok seemed to already know all about Dept. Head Kim. He even told us a story about how Dept. Head Kim once berated a cleaning lady before brazenly unzipping his pants to relieve himself in the adjacent urinal without waiting for her to finish cleaning. I also thought of an incident I'd never told anyone about. It was the time that he looked at Team Leader Yu and said with a frown that she would look a lot better with a different hairstyle and color of lipstick. Despite complaining to me about the comment, Team Leader Yu never filed a complaint and instead changed both her hairstyle and lipstick, just as he'd implied she should do. But I wanted to respect her privacy, so I decided not to use this story as bar talk.

One time, unable to bear seeing her treated that way, I asked her why she didn't fight back.

"He's so rude. You should kick him in the crotch or something."

"Jihye, I have two kids. Putting up with his comments are how I ensure that he'll say yes when I ask to leave on time, when I ask to use my PTO to stay home with my kids when they have a fever. You have to pick your battles. Someday you'll learn that."

"But Team Leader Yu, this is wrong. Hasn't it ever occurred to you that what Dept. Head Kim is doing is sexual harassment?"

"If you have a problem with it, why don't you take it up with him? Why are you complaining to me?"

Team Leader Yu asked this quietly. Her eyes were serious, and I could tell she wasn't mad at me. She gave me a smile before patting me on the back and leaving.

I was lost for words. Perhaps there was a good but incomprehensible reason—incomprehensible at least to me—for why she always talked about it being impossible for her to communicate with people who didn't have children. Perhaps it wasn't a choice. Perhaps the problem was a system that had worn her down slowly until it changed the way she thought about the world. Indeed, if she had said something true but irreverent to Dept. Head Kim, she would lose favor with him. And when that happened, he would have made her life miserable until she eventually quit. And once that happened, she wouldn't have been able to provide for her children.

"Should we show him who's boss?" Gyuok said. "Just as a test. To see if shameless people really never feel ashamed."

Little did I know, these weren't just the ramblings of a man who'd had a little too much to drink.

7

I THINK I'M SEEING
THE LIGHT

The incident occurred just a few days later as I walked into the office to start work. Everyone was chatting noisily, a cup of coffee in their hand to chase away the sleep. Everyone, that is, except for Dept. Head Kim. He was by himself at his desk and looking down at something. As I got closer, I could make out his expression better: a stony face, his jaw dangling from his skull.

I wasn't the only one who noticed this.

"What's wrong?" Team Leader Yu asked as she went over to him.

Dept. Head Kim pointed to something, his finger trembling.

"Someone's . . . got a weird sense of humor . . ."

On his desk was a piece of A4 paper, intentionally crumpled and spread flat again to give it a weathered appearance. The letter was composed in the style of a ransom note with colorful cutouts of letters from magazines to hide the culprit's identity. It almost looked like a child's art project, had it not been for the contents of the letter.

STOP FARTING.

COVER YOUR BURPS.

BUY ANTI-DANDRUFF SHAMPOO.

PITIFUL SWINE!

In the corner was a drawing of a pig's head, above which was a speech bubble with the words "oink oink." Team Leader Yu let out a gasp as she brought her palm to her mouth. Blue in the face, Dept. Head Kim turned to glare at her.

"Is this your doing, Team Leader Yu?"

"It wasn't me!"

Appalled that he would accuse her of such a thing, Team Leader Yu's eyebrows suddenly changed from surprised to indignant as she fell back into her chair, expelling the air from the cushion with a *poof*. I couldn't help myself from turning to look at Gyuok, who was minding his own business as he changed a light bulb.

He must have sensed my gaze because he turned toward the group and asked in a cheery tone, "Did something happen?" No one knew how to answer him without a long explanation that would only embarrass Dept. Head Kim even more.

The air in the office was a few degrees cooler for the rest of the day. Lunch was spent in solemn silence, too, and Dept. Head Kim got up from his chair and hurried out of the restaurant without even finishing half of his food. But to my surprise, not once during the meal did he break wind or burp. He also refrained from picking his teeth at the table. No one could really enjoy their meal. In fact, the only one who seemed to have an appetite was Gyuok, who ordered twice the amount he usually ate. We made eye contact several times as he spooned food into his mouth, but the expression he wore on his face never changed. He even had the brazenness to jokingly ask me, "Why do you keep staring at me? If you want a bite, all you gotta do is ask."

I stayed behind after everyone but Gyuok left the restaurant, waiting for my chance to speak with him.

"Don't you think you've gone too far? And when did you have the time to put it there anyway?"

Gyuok let out a groan as he stretched, bending his neck from side to side.

"I came in early this morning."

"Have you lost your mind? They have security cameras in the office, you know. You don't think they'll catch you?"

I was speaking in a hushed voice, but Gyuok didn't bother to lower his volume.

"You really think they're going to check the security cameras over a harmless prank? There's a whole process for obtaining security footage. I doubt Dept. Head Kim wants to bring any more attention to the letter than he needs to. Anyway, we're out of good whiteboard markers. Order some new ones, would ya?"

He gave me a close-lipped grin.

To my amazement, there was no attempt to find the culprit, just as Gyuok had predicted. In fact, the only change I noticed was the improved air quality in the office. Come to think of it, I hadn't heard or smelled Dept. Head Kim's flatulence since the incident. On the third day after it happened, he started coming to work with his lunches packed and was noticeably more reticent. And whenever he asked for a favor, the expression on his face wasn't his usual arrogant smirk, but a sheepish smile. Of course, there was this feeling of mistrust in the air now, but I'd take that over methane and hydrogen sulfide any day.

And yet, what had changed about our situation? We were still just glorified part-time workers masquerading as interns. Low-paid, non-regular workers who copied documents and ran errands. But the incident with Dept. Head Kim did serve as an inflection point, not for my circumstances but for my view of Gyuok. The fact that there was a secret between us that no one else in the office knew made me feel a secret sense of solidarity with him. Every once in a while, I'd catch myself staring at him out of the corner of my eye.

He always smiled when he made eye contact with someone, no matter who it was. His smile was equitable and gentle, filled with goodwill. And yet, I knew almost nothing about him, even though he sat right next to me. I had a feeling that I'd never get to know him unless I was willing to confront him, to tell him I knew it was all an act. So one evening when it looked like we wouldn't have to work late, I decided to ask him the question I'd had on the tip of my tongue for weeks.

"Why did you make a scene that day at the café with Professor Park?"

I stuttered as I explained to him how I knew about him and the professor, and as I did this, I could feel my face getting red-hot. I knew *I* hadn't done anything wrong, but for some reason the blood rushed through the capillaries in my face and perspiration collected on the back of my neck. My body always reacted this way when I was nervous. I would stutter and lose the ability to think.

"And then there was that prank you played on Dept. Head Kim. What are you trying to accomplish?"

It took all my strength just to finish. Instead of answering my question, Gyuok looked me straight in the eye in a way that made me think he thought this amusing.

"Do you want to know about *me* or do you want to know what I'm trying to *do*?"

"Both. I don't think you can really separate the two."

I couldn't have expected what Gyuok was going to say next.

"Why don't we get to know each other over drinks? Just the two of us."

There was that polar bear again, beaming at me. *Just the two of us.* If he hadn't said these five words in that soft voice of his, I wouldn't have gone with him for drinks that night.

* * *

Flowing out of the speakers was Benny Goodman's "Body and Soul." Either by design or by mistake, this one song had been playing on endless repeat since we arrived. I could see six empty beer bottles on our table, but I could hardly remember a single thing we'd talked about. We were just existing, speechless and in a dream state, letting the tune trickle in and out of our ears. Sometimes, when the music, alcohol, and emotions were just right, no words were needed.

Sitting in front of me was an average man dressed in loose jeans and a T-shirt with a collar which had seen better days. An intern who dusted the company's electrical cords and played pranks on people in positions of power. He was unusually light-skinned for a Korean man, and his facial features, although a bit plain, were in perfect harmony with each other. He wasn't my type; in fact, he shared almost nothing in common with the men I'd dated. And yet, I was having trouble categorizing the emotions I felt toward him. My shoulder was still tingling from when he'd touched it, guiding me into the bar from the alley. This can't be! I gave my brain a firm shake. But I couldn't deny the pulsations in my chest. Perhaps it had something to do with the fact that he always made an effort to say my name at the end of every sentence when talking to me. "Ms. Jihye, Ms. Jihye—"

"Is it okay if I keep calling you Ms. Jihye?" he asked out of nowhere as though he were reading my mind. "If you think that's too informal, should I call you sunbae instead?"

"No. I mean, we're both interns after all. And in terms of age, we were born the same year."

"I guess you're right. We're the same age."

We looked at each other and started reminiscing about the past.

"Do you remember ninety-four?" he asked. "I was in preschool. They extended summer break for weeks because of the heat waves that year."

"I remember people used to joke that the temperature on the thermometer and the year on the calendar were the same number, but I don't remember anything else. I do remember, however, the IMF crisis happening when I was in third grade. My uncle had to come back from studying abroad, and my mom sold her gold ring to help the gold-collection campaign. Did they really think that selling their gold was going to save the country?"

"We entered junior high just at the turn of the century. Remember that song by Lee Jung-hyun? 'Change, change, change everything.' Studying for the junior high school entrance exam, memorizing the quadratic formula. All I wanted was for the world to end."

"That must have been when everyone was eating Fin.K.L bread and collecting Pokémon ddakji."

"Yeah, yeah. And everyone was talking about the end of the world. People were losing their minds, talking about the Rapture and 'rising to the clouds to meet the Lord.' The same thing happened in 2012. But here we are. I guess the world is more stubborn than people give it credit for."

We snickered together as we reminisced about the past—what it was like to witness Kim Yuna's first Olympics, who was the more passionate Super Junior fan, how we spent every day customizing our Cyworld profiles, and the cringey memories from our rebellious teenage years. We also talked about what happened to our favorite actors from *Sharp*, especially Lee Eun-sung, who'd surprised everyone by marrying the famous singer, Seo Taiji. And then there was, of course, G-Dragon, the most successful Korean who'd been born in 1988.

"They were turbulent times. I feel like we've been through so much."

This made Gyuok wave his finger at me, as though what I said was gravely wrong.

"You call that turbulent? Our grandparents were born under Japanese colonial rule and had to flee on trains from a civil war that split the country in two. They were well into middle age before witnessing the Miracle on the Han River. I was in a taxi once when an Audi cut in front of us. The taxi driver started swearing up a storm, going on and on about how he'd fought in Vietnam. 'You're lucky I don't still have my M60! Kids these days have no respect for veterans.' His veins were popping out of his neck. I thought we were going to get into an accident with the way he was chasing after that Audi."

"So what happened after that?" I asked.

"Not wanting to be a bystander to road rage, I decided to thank him for his service to the country. And not just military. I said it's because of people like him that South Korea became so prosperous. It's true. You can't deny that we wouldn't be here today without men like him. Thankfully, that seemed to calm him down."

"But sometimes I wonder. You know how we always criticize and pity older generations. But I wonder if I would have done differently if I were in their position. It's easy to fault people, to hold everyone up to the same standards of dignity, morality, and common sense. But people are inherently selfish, and in extreme situations, it becomes the duty of the few to maintain dignity, morality, and common sense. Is there any way I can guarantee that I wouldn't have become exactly the same if I'd been born back then and gone through the same history they had to go through? And if I can't, maybe I'm the one who needs to try a little harder."

"What do you mean?"

"At the very least, I need to constantly vow that I won't just fight for my own share. It's over the moment I become selfish. I don't know what the right answer is. All I hope is that little by little, I'm heading in the right direction."

We had come here to learn about each other, but as of yet, we hadn't really shared any personal information. Nevertheless, I welcomed the sense of solidarity with someone from my generation, someone with whom I could talk about these things and not worry about getting criticized.

Suddenly feeling my face get hot again, I took a large swig of beer, using the beer bottle to cover my face. Even though I couldn't see his eyes, I could tell that he was staring intently at me. Could I be honest with him? I must be drunk just for thinking this.

"I still haven't answered your question. You want to know how I know Professor Park."

"Actually, you told everyone in the café how you know each other. And I already know that you helped him write his book, and that you weren't paid for any of it. What I want to know is why you acted the way you did. In front of everyone like that. Why make a scene?"

After I said this, I had to swallow all the saliva that was accumulating in my mouth. Gyuok stared off in the distance for a while before answering.

"I couldn't sleep. I basically wrote that book. No one believes me, though. I knew I was doing the wrong thing, but I tricked my conscience into helping him. A friend had told me about the job, and at first, I was just helping him organize documents. Once I realized what happened, I was so filled with regret. And that regret eventually turned into anger. One way or another, he had to lose something. Even if it was just a momentary loss of dignity. That was the only way it would be a little fair. After all, he had done something wrong, and he was able to keep his dignity without paying anything in return."

"You did it to punish him?"

"Not as punishment. Something closer to humiliation. That's what I wanted to give him. Twenty years ago, when he did that horrible thing to that girl, everyone thought he wouldn't be able to show his face again. But the exact opposite happened. He didn't even switch fields. In fact, he became a bestselling author writing and philosophizing about the very sexual depravity that got him in trouble in the first place. How can that be? I just wanted to shout from the top of a mountain that this is wrong. I can't say what difference it made. But after I got back at Professor Park for cheating me out of recognition and money, I didn't know what to do next. I was searching for something to do when one day, I discovered a job posting on the home page of the academy he'd been working at. So, I applied. You could say that it's thanks to him that I'm working here."

Gyuok let out a bitter laugh as he gave the beer bottle in his hand a swirl.

"But it's funny. After I did that to Professor Park, the burning sensation in my chest disappeared. All I did was yell a few words in a café. But it occurred to me that at the very least I'd made him meditate on the shame lying dormant in his mind. I started thinking a lot after that. Perhaps the world changes just a little bit, even when all you do is call out injustice for what it is."

"I envy you. And your courage. I'd never be able to do that. Even when I know someone should speak up, I've never been the one to act. It's not that I can't. At least I think it's because I choose not to. But is there really a difference? I'm another face in the audience. That's the kind of person I am. At least I find comfort in the fact that I'm not the only one, that most people are like me."

Gyuok gently reached over and clinked his bottle against mine.

"What's a lead actor without his audience? It's the masses that make the artist, not the other way around. Of course, perhaps there are some artists who think that art can stay hidden in a room, away from the eyes of the public, and still be considered art."

I let out a loud, short laugh. But no sooner did I do this than I realized it wasn't that funny.

"To put it differently, you're amazing, Ms. Jihye. Precisely because you're in the audience and part of the masses."

"Thank you but that doesn't really make me feel any better. People say that the universe is all made of dust. But I've never felt happy about being called space dust."

"You won't get anywhere thinking like that. Anyone can go up on stage if they want to. The only reason the audience doesn't is because they don't think about it. But—"

Gyuok opened and closed his fist a few times.

"That's exactly what we need. If someone doesn't act, the world won't change."

"It'll take a lot more than action."

"Are you so sure about that? If there's one thing I know, it's that if the world hasn't changed, it means someone didn't act."

That was the contraposition of his earlier statement. As I pondered whether this was right, he asked me something unexpected.

"But what do you *really* want to do, Ms. Jihye?"

This felt overly confrontational, so much so that it almost felt insulting. What do you *really* want to do? Who would feel comfortable receiving that question? In fact, I'd spent my whole life avoiding this exact question, afraid of the answer "I don't know." And here I was. I'd been running from the knowledge that my once closely held dreams had become a distant reality. But it was too late. What was the point of bringing up old aspirations if all it led to was regret? I began to speak slowly.

"Something different. You know, not the art and literature pushed by large corporations. Something with variety, something worthwhile, however small it may be. Something that people appreciate despite its small scope, but not that garbage published in small pamphlets, pretending to be high art just because it's fringe. I wanted it to be my job to think about art and bring it to people. It's because of that dream that I've been bouncing around from company to company with all this student debt. But at some point, I realized I'd reached my limit."

I exhaled a small sigh.

"And you know what? After all of that, I was still applying for positions at large companies. In the end, corporations control everything, even cultural production. They get the results they want because they have the money to make it work. Anything can look appetizing to people if you pump enough capital into it. What I'm trying to say is, in order to do what I wanted, I had to compromise my values. Why? Because they have all the power and I have none."

"And then?"

"And then I started falling behind. One rejection after another. And all the while, I was throwing my money away on English lessons and Starbucks. And when I did finally get hired, it was at this academy, a subsidiary of yet another large company. So here I am, sitting in front of you, pretending that my working here longer makes me more qualified, while I talk about how I've failed to become part of the mainstream."

Silence fell between us. Gyuok was giving me a strange look. Was it compassion? A sense of comradery perhaps? I brought the bottle of beer to my mouth and took a slow, long sip. The bubbling of the carbonation tickled the mucus membranes of my esophagus. How did we get on this topic? It'd been too long since the question was asked for me to remember.

"Thanks for letting me in. You know, I want to talk more. With you, Ms. Jihye."

I lifted my head. He was staring intently at me again. A smile was starting to spread across his face. But his eyes were looking through me. A husky voice sounded from the entrance.

"Hey, Ms. Wise! I didn't expect to see you here."

It was Muin and Mr. Nam. I realized that Gyuok's smile hadn't been for me. He'd been welcoming our two friends. My face turned bright red as I realized I'd turned into Yeong-sook from *Madame Anemone*. Mr. Nam and Muin each took a seat in the chairs next to us.

"Sorry we're late," Mr. Nam said. "It ended later than expected."

"We had to meet up before coming here. Hey, this is a cool bar," Muin said.

"I hope we weren't interrupting a conversation between two lovebirds." Mr. Nam glanced back and forth between me and Gyuok.

"A date?" Gyuok said, waving his hands in the air. "Don't insult Ms. Jihye. We were just talking about life."

I felt somewhat betrayed and flustered by the way he revealed and trivialized the secret conversation we'd just been having. But why were Muin and Mr. Nam here anyway?

"So, I heard that you really put that letter on your department head's desk."

"Well, I have no beef with him, personally. But I'm sure it made Ms. Jihye happy."

"Well, the air in the office is cleaner now, at least."

I hadn't meant this to be funny, but everyone burst out laughing.

"This is just the start. Right now, everything looks like a harmless prank. But it's not meaningless. Somehow, someway, this is going to change us."

Gyuok was going on without making much sense. And yet, the other two looked completely in to what he was preaching.

"Exactly," Mr. Nam said. "And even if nothing comes of this, it's still a hell of a lot more exciting than sitting around and doing nothing."

"I agree," Muin said as he picked at his lip. "I've got a lot on my mind and nothing to do. Apart from my part-time job at the convenience store and the two high school students I tutor in writing, of course. I'll participate in whatever way I can."

"Participate . . . ?"

It seemed I was the only one out of the loop. Gyuok's thick eyelashes fluttered.

"I want to have some fun. The world's become stiff and rigid. Everyone's suffering from lethargy. I want to start a revolution. I want to be defiant. I don't care if they call me immature. History tells us that radical revolutions always fail, and the world is getting smaller by the day. If we're seen, we're bound to get squashed or suppressed. I want to start a movement that can't be squashed or suppressed. Something fun. Like a prank."

"A prank?"

I asked this cautiously, feeling like there was a large gap between the word "prank" and the letter that he'd left on Dept. Head Kim's desk. Gyuok explained that we needed pranks to bring about change. We needed to give the middle finger to injustice. And if we kept at it, eventually something would change. That was his argument. It was the kind of thing that made sense when you first heard it but didn't stand up to logic once you really thought about it. Mr. Nam brought his fist down on the table as if to settle the matter.

"We're talking too much. I don't know exactly what you mean for us to do, but if it's going to be fun, I'm in. What about you, Muin?"

Muin nodded his head. "Anything to stimulate my old brain."

Gyuok's eyes gently turned toward me.

"I guess I still haven't asked you. Ms. Jihye, do you want to do this together?"

All of them were waiting for my answer, but I couldn't give it to them.

"What we're going to do might seem trite and ridiculous. But even the smallest of practical jokes can cause a storm. Just don't get your expectations up. That's all I'm saying. It's the act itself that's our goal. Just have fun."

Gyuok finished the rest of his beer in one shot. The quick dance music in the bar switched back to old jazz as I watched his Adam's apple move up and down. Ella Fitzgerald's drowsy rendition of "I'm Beginning to See the Light" gently caressed my ears. I didn't know whether Gyuok's plans would show me the light; all I wanted was to stop walking in place. I wanted to go somewhere, it didn't matter where. At some point during his long explanation, I interrupted him by muttering to myself:

"Me too. I want to do this together."

I stressed the word "together" despite not knowing what it was we would be doing. The corners of Gyuok's mouth curled slightly. The alcohol in our veins was slowly becoming more concentrated. The air danced and the world spun round and round. Enveloped by jazzy tunes, our voices were getting louder and louder. Ella was going on and on about how she was beginning to see the light. I gently closed my eyes. I knew for sure they were shut, but I could have sworn I saw a light flickering somewhere in the distance.

8

DANCING ON ASHES

I was never one to act. I was the kind of person who hid and laid low. But the waves of revolution swept through South Korea when I was a freshman in college. It felt like the '80s all over again, even though we were nearing the 2010s. Cherry blossoms were falling, and summer was in the air. Across the nation, people took to the streets with candles in hand. Everyone stayed up late into the night, singing songs and taunting the police and their water cannons. I was one of the many who joined the protests.

Every day we gathered in the plaza like it was a festival, bound together by a sense of long-awaited, cross-generational unity. And yet, while everyone else was filled with hope and a sense of duty, I felt lost, my mind scattered like dark rain clouds on the horizon. The feeling of failure after being rejected twice by all the prestigious universities I had applied to, and the feeling of listlessness after breaking up with my first real boyfriend, were too heavy a burden for a nineteen-year-old girl. I didn't know what I was doing there with all those people. I knew I'd be missing out if I wasn't where the action was, and I knew instinctively that this was a cause that I agreed with, even though I really didn't know why or how. But the candle in my hand had no power, and the flag representing my university, which was located on the outskirts of the capital, looked embarrassingly shoddy compared to the proudly fluttering flags of the prestigious universities.

So one day, I slipped away from the march. Even the noisiest of places have dead spots, so it didn't take me long to find somewhere quiet. I climbed up the inner wall of the residential complex across from the plaza. It was quiet and dark. Shouting and singing sounded in the distance. The aroma of candle smoke rode to my nose on waves of air currents. Sitting there alone, I made a promise to myself never to forget this moment, when I was alone while everyone gathered in the plaza. Most of all, I wanted that moment to remain nameless. I didn't want it to become a memory of the collective but a lonely fragment of a beautiful panorama that I'd keep for myself.

Sitting on that wall, I had a rather sad premonition. Everyone was going to forget today. The passion of this moment was nothing but a fleeting flash of fireworks.

The protests failed in the end. I was amazed at how fast everything became mere reminiscences. All those people went back to their own lives to live only for themselves.

Drunk from all the beer, I said goodbye to everyone at the bar and went home to sit in front of my computer and search for pictures of that summer when people from across the country marched through the plaza. I was always amazed when I saw the images of tens of thousands of candles filling the street outside Gwanghwamun Gate. A wave of light gaining momentum one photon at a time to change the world. Pure and beautiful. Had such a thing really happened? And where among all those lit candles was I? I felt a rush of emotions, strong and volatile.

But no matter how angry and indignant people feel, they are always quick to forget the outrageous yet commonplace things that made them angry and indignant in the first place. Perhaps that's the only way people get on with their lives. They can't live if they don't forget.

I was one of many. Following the crowd, doing what everyone else was doing. I chose what most people chose, did what most people did, didn't do what most people didn't do. Faced with the popular opinion, I usually nodded my head or agreed reluctantly.

So why did I agree to Gyuok's proposal? It wasn't just because I was attracted to him. For once, just this once, I wanted to scream out with confidence. I want to tell everyone that I was different from them.

* * *

It was a dark and wet evening. The location of our first shenanigan was an underpass near Hongdae, Seoul's youngest and most artsy district. The gray concrete wall was covered in graffiti. Muin pulled out of his backpack the spray cans he'd brought.

"My old roommate made a name for himself as a graffiti artist. He left these when he moved out."

We stared at the wall for a moment. English words that I didn't understand, pictures of robots, and faces upon faces.

"Well, let's get started," Gyuok said.

Mr. Nam seemed reluctant. "But we're not professionals. Are you sure we can do this?"

"That's the point. This is practice. We're training ourselves to break the obedience for authority that's taken root inside of us."

"What's graffiti got to do with authority?"

"Graffiti at its core is a resistance against authority. That's where it came from. When you bring together a bunch of formless scribblings and give them meaning, you make new culture. But look at this."

Gyuok pointed to a section of the wall on which the portrait of a man had been painted. You could tell immediately that this work had been done with great care, even the quality of the spray paint used looked better than the other graffiti.

"The painting is whatever. It's *this* that I have a problem with."

Gyuok drew our attention to the words beneath the portrait.

I put my heart and soul into this.
Please don't erase so others can enjoy.

Written beneath this were the artist's credentials, his name, even his alma mater. The name looked familiar.

"Do you know who this is? He's a relatively famous modern artist. They say that he brought students here to paint the background for him. He said he was 'lending' his talents to the next generation. And then he has the audacity to write a warning to others, telling them not to erase his work because he put effort into it. The essence of street art is freedom. But even here, someone is trying to exercise authority."

Gyuok stopped talking. I played devil's advocate.

"But Basquiat puts copyright marks on his graffiti. He says it's an expression of his pride as an artist."

"You're right. But he's never asked people not to *erase* his works.

And this underpass, for the last several decades it's been the people's canvas. Anyone can paint here. Not only did he put up a sign forbidding people from painting over his work, but he also uploaded a video of himself giving an interview in front of the wall, complete with links to purchase his art. For a graffiti artist, that's essentially admitting you have no talent. It's like putting up a 'Do not walk on grass' sign in a public park."

I remembered I'd once read about the origin of graffiti. There were various theories, including one that claimed its origins went all the way back to cave paintings. Whatever the case, it was TAKI 183 who first popularized the art form. In the early 1970s, the tag TAKI 183 was discovered all over New York. No one knew what it meant or who was doing it, and slowly people started referring to the mysterious artist as TAKI 183. When his identity was finally revealed, he was nothing but an unassuming postman, and 183 simply referred to his street address. He'd started the tradition as a way to leave traces of himself at the places he went for work. All because he wanted to, because he thought it'd be fun. That's how graffiti was born, not as some form of art, but as a fragment of the landscape.

Thanks to him, graffiti became known as street art, art on the frontier. But soon, it became a headache for the city of New York, and people started doubting its artistic value. It wasn't until the anonymous art-terrorist Banksy that graffiti was brought back into serious discussions about art.

Banksy, whose identity is protected by a mask, is famous for turning shabby walls into pieces of art. With beautiful and powerful paintings and humorous statements, he points out what's wrong with the world. The people who at first showed disdain for the works eventually welcomed Banksy and expressed respect. They even put his works onto canvases to be displayed at exhibitions in his name. He became so popular that he had to express his dissatisfaction with the commercialization of his works. But in the sense that he moved people's hearts, he succeeded. But what about me? Standing in front of that intimidating wall, I didn't know what I was to do.

As I was lost in thought, I heard a jet of aerosol next to me. It was Muin. He was spraying long streaks above the artist's precious work. He drew three long lines horizontally, then four lines vertically intersecting these lines. Then, after putting a little slash at the top left-hand corner of the grid, he punctuated the piece with four dots.

無

Nonexistence. He then wrote the character for "person" next to this.

無人

"I've forgotten most of my Hanja education, but this much I can read," Mr. Nam said. "Mu-in: person who doesn't exist. Muin, don't tell me that's actually what your name means."

"It's pronounced the same, but no. My name means benevolent fighter. I used these characters instead because people treat me like I don't exist."

We stared at the large character for nonexistence that he'd painted.

"Now that I look at it, the character mu is really geometrical. Why would you need such a complicated character to represent nonexistence?"

"The four dots at the bottom of the character are supposed to represent ashes. They're the ashes after a fire has burned down a forest, leaving nothing behind," Muin said.

"So philosophical. I reckon a circle would have done the trick."

Mr. Nam clicked his tongue as he spray-painted a circle.

"Hey, this is kind of fun. Ms. Wise, you should try it too."

While Mr. Nam made hearts, stars, and other simple shapes, I took my can and shook it. I brought it up to the wall and pressed down on the nozzle with my finger. I could feel the vibrations in my fingertips as the aerosolized paint was ejected from the nozzle. It tingled. I didn't know what to write. So I just drew lines over the words and pictures that filled the wall surface. Thick particles slowly started covering the other graffiti. In my life, I was the kind of person who could cover no one, who could erase no one. It was exhilarating that the spray can in my hand was doing this for me. Although, in some ways, it was also a bit depressing.

I glanced over at Gyuok. Unlike Mr. Nam, who was going to town on the wall, Gyuok stared at the wall for a long time before deciding to paint a mustache on the artist's smug portrait. Muin seemed the most serious. Even after everyone was done, he was still hunched over painting something. He finally stepped back and said, "Ta-da!" He'd changed "nonexistence" to "dance."

"What, you're a dancer now?"

Muin nodded his head as he pointed to the strokes that had replaced the dots.

"Do you know what this part means? It's pronounced cheon (舛) and it means to disturb. Dancing atop the ashes of a forest will disturb them and cast them to the wind. That's the sense in which I'm going to dance."

He started moving his body as if trying to dance. In the distance, I could hear an old Korean pop song. Mr. Nam began to dance, too, swaying left and right like a roly-poly toy.

Gyuok extended his hand toward me in a stately manner.

"Sophia, may I have this dance?"

A gave him a coy look before taking his hand. As our clumsy steps became more relaxed, a gust of wind blew through the underpass. The headlights of a car passing by flashed across the tunnel, bringing our shadows into existence for a brief moment. And my heart became light as air and floated into the sky.

I waited a week before returning to the underpass by myself. Our art had already been painted over by other artists. It looked like my lines had been covered up for quite some time. But Muin's piece had survived. Written around it like a sign of approval was a large star and other derivative pieces. At least one trace of us remained. Dance. I knew that this too would soon be painted over, but the fact that it had lasted this long was enough. I took a picture with my cell phone and sent it to everyone. Muin seemed overjoyed and sent a reply that surprised me.

—I'm sitting at my desk right now. I'm going to try to write again. Writers gotta write!

9

A MOTHER AND A FATHER

*I*t's been forever since I've had a drink!"

Dabin whispered this to herself as she hoisted a foamy glass of beer up to her lips, tears forming in her eyes. But just before she could take her first sip, the part-time waiter ran over with a concerned look on his face, asking to see Dabin's ID. Dabin rolled her eyes as she pulled out the card and handed it to him. The waiter stood there speechless for a moment before handing it back. Five feet two, ninety-two pounds, with short hair and a round baby face—Dabin could hardly pass for a high school student, let alone an adult. Dabin and I, along with three others, had all been relatively close back in college. We would take classes together, were always the first to tell one another about a new boyfriend, and for a while after graduation, continued to meet up whenever someone was celebrating a birthday.

But as we entered our midtwenties, differences in our lifestyles and privilege started to creep up here and there. The glue that held us together had been cracking bit by bit until finally Jiwon's marriage (the first in our friend group) ripped the friendships wide open. Jiwon was from a well-to-do family and was in no rush to enter the job market after college, instead spending her time dating and shopping. But then one day she announced that she had gotten engaged. Once the date was set, she began posting pictures of diamond rings and dresses and makeup and bedsheets for her new home, asking us for our opinion, even though no one except her had expensive enough tastes to see a difference between the choices. Pictures that, mind you, we'd already seen because she'd posted them to her Instagram. But that was only the beginning. The real problem was that Dabin, who had gotten engaged around the same time as Jiwon, resented Jiwon and her vanity.

Dabin was a pragmatist. In college, she'd studied her butt off so that her parents wouldn't have to help her financially. And with her fiancé, she'd agreed to split payments for their house fifty-fifty, and even broke the tradition of yemul, rejecting the customary exchanging of gifts between the bride and groom's families. Hearing this, Jiwon, who was anything but pragmatic, would tell Dabin that she was entering a disadvantageous marriage and that her fiancé wasn't carrying his weight, that he took her for granted.

The situation was so uncomfortable that the four of us created our own KakaoTalk chat room without Jiwon. As a result, the old chat room became a sort of mausoleum for product links and pictures, its halls echoing with the sound of unanswered messages. Understandably, Jiwon lost it when the secret got out. The fight started with everyone arguing about what was said and how, and eventually deteriorated into name-calling and cheap personal attacks. Jiwon even took to social media, where every day she posted toxic tweets directed at one or all of us. We all stayed friends just long enough to attend Jiwon's wedding, but once the party was over, there was no fixing the friendships. I hadn't talked to Yuri and Hyena in years, but remained close with Dabin, whose down-to-earth values were much closer to mine—as least compared to Jiwon, who looked down on people for how much, or actually how little, they spent on their wedding.

Most everyone has that one story of heroism and great personal strug-gle that made them who they are; for Dabin, that story used to be about that one time she went to Australia on a "working holiday" yet she almost died from being overworked. But not anymore. Now the story was one of married life and parenthood. I'd been truly shocked when Dabin first announced her engagement. I was positive that she would be the last to get married, if not the only one who stayed single forever. She said she'd gotten married young because it gave her better options. "In that sense," she added, "I'm no different from Jiwon."

While in Australia, Dabin was treated like a machine. She worked all day under the hot sun, competing against other field hands while being exploited by middle managers and a shameless landowner who viewed all his workers as disposable. Whenever I listened to her story, I wondered if she hadn't accidentally become a modern-day serf.

So when I thought about how she accepted her boyfriend's proposal without hesitation, despite the fact that she hadn't really done anything with her life yet, I sometimes wondered if it wasn't because she used up all her youthful energy on that farm in the outback. Whatever the reason, the marriage resulted in a resignation letter to the travel agency she'd been working at since coming back from Australia and a son, who was now in preschool.

And so here she was, chugging beer from a glass big enough to dwarf her own head while she vented to me at a bar about the stress of raising her son by herself and her inability to communicate with her husband. To me, Dabin's life story seemed terribly cliché, and yet she kept repeating the phrase "That's life," as if her situation was universal to all women with a husband and child. She'd been steely when we'd first sat down, but now that she had enough alcohol in her system, she was talking up a storm as though all she needed was a big dose of ethanol to recharge her battery.

"It was a living nightmare until he turned three. I'd try to get up after waiting an hour for him to fall asleep in my arms, but the sound of my aching back would wake him up and he'd start crying again all over again. It was like that twenty-four seven. After a while, I started to hear things. I would imagine him crying while watching TV, and sometimes I got this strange sound in my ear. Sometimes it was like metal on metal. And sometimes it was the sound of waves. After several long years, I finally made him into a functioning human being who can go to the bathroom and dress himself. And now that he's five, it's like suddenly, he's a teenager, always cranky and pushing me away whenever I try to help him." Dabin let out a long sigh. "Sorry. I used to hate hearing women complain about how hard life is after becoming a mother. But now I know what they were talking about. It's not just the aches and pains or the lack of sleep. I can never do what I want to do. All I want is a few moments of peace. A few seconds by myself in the bathroom. A meal that I can enjoy alone. An uninterrupted drink of water from the fridge. But everything gets interrupted by the sound of crying and whining, and then I need to start whatever I was doing all over again. A woman goes crazy under those conditions. At the farm, all I had to do was work fast and adapt. It was exhausting, sure, but all I had to do was push through the pain and work a little bit harder. That's not the case with children. It's the worst form of psychological torture. I know now why women in the old days would go to work in the fields with their babies on their backs. At least that way, they had something to distract themselves while babysitting. And then there's my asshole of a husband . . ."

She abruptly stopped talking to chug some more beer.

"But what's the point? It's such a banal story, I hate telling it."

She began laughing in an unhinged manner. Saying she wanted to talk about something more uplifting, she told me stories about Australia, about the pervert at her part-time job in college, and the time she was on TV to compete in a singing competition, all the while laughing and reminiscing about the good ole days. Back then, her hair had been dyed all manner of hues and colors. All of it had happened only a few years ago, but the way she talked, you'd think these things had happened in another lifetime.

"But you don't look like you've aged a day. You still get carded at bars. No one would look at you and think you're a mother." I tried to ignore the dark bags beneath her eyes as I said this.

Dabin shook her head in an exaggerated manner. "I've become a completely different person. Of course raising a family has brought me a lot of happiness and satisfaction. But I've changed. I'm much more conservative. My main priorities are my son's safety and the well-being of my family. I make civil complaints to the local borough and call the police for the smallest of things. I'll do it even if it's just a bunch of noisy high schoolers playing outside while I'm trying to put my son to sleep. To think that just a few years ago, I was one of those noisy kids. Do you know how people become

conservative? It happens the moment they have something to protect. It happens as soon as people have something they don't want
to have taken away, something they don't want people coming in
and ruining. A house, money, a way of life. For me, it's my son. Once
I gave birth to him, I suddenly saw danger at every corner. I used
to be so arrogant, always turning my nose up at worldly concerns,
but now all I think about is traffic accidents, war, psychopaths, endocrine disruptors, and air pollution. I feel like I need to protect
my family and home from everything that's out there in the world.
And it's this way of thinking that has pushed me to become more
and more conservative. I have trouble understanding people who
aren't like me. I look at everything with a distrusting eye. I assume
everything is a threat to me and my family. But I still wonder how
I became like this. I'm barely thirty. I thought Australia was bad. I
had no idea what being a mother would do to me."

Dabin, who looked like she wouldn't be able to pass a field so-
briety test, suddenly jumped to her feet.

"Well, I think I've had enough fun. I'm going."

"So suddenly? I thought we were going to stay up all night."

"I've got to get home and get some sleep. We're busy these days
with preparing for EK."

"EK?"

"English kindergarten. I've got to make him study for his level test."

"Study? What five-year-old studies?"

"They have to take a level test to sort children into classes. If he
does poorly, he'll be put into the inferior class."

The Dabin I knew was against the establishment and said she
would never send her child to academies and cram schools to
study until midnight like everyone else. She had been your typical

twentysomething-year-old Korean: staunchly liberal and deeply dissatisfied with Korean society and its inability to change. It was she who had said she didn't care about expensive weddings and tradition. It was she who called weddings a vanity fair, who only consented to having one because her parents insisted. I couldn't believe the woman standing in front of me talking about making her five-year-old son study English was the same Dabin I knew from before.

"I told you. I'm a conservative now, and that means I've come to accept and understand why things are the way they are. I have no choice but to send him to English cram school. It's not just for his studies. Cram schools are like day cares. They're the only way a mother can get some respite. And if I start doing everything on my own and acting like I'm better than everyone else, I'll have to prepare myself to be shunned from the mother-student community in my neighborhood, and they're my only way to stay connected. You don't know how cruel and conniving mothers can be. I don't want it to affect my son. You think I'm just exaggerating. I thought the same way when I used to watch those documentaries about our school system. I used to think Koreans were crazy for deferring college for a year or two just because they want to retake their exams and get into a better school. But now that it's my daily reality, I realize people aren't just being overdramatic."

I had nothing to say. It was a world I had no clue about, a world I didn't *want* to have a clue about. And yet, I couldn't help but wonder: Would I have done the same if I were in her position? It bothered me that I couldn't say no with confidence.

"I spent 14 million won to go on a working holiday. Why? To learn English. But you know what? I can't speak a word of English in front of those little brats at our local English academy. At the very least, I want to make sure my son doesn't suffer because he can't speak English. People are saying we might not need to study other languages in the future because of AI, but they don't know for sure. My hands are tied. The most obvious thing that I can do for him right now is send him to a kindergarten where they speak English."

Dabin paused for a moment, as if noticing my staring, and then she said this:

"It must be nice to have so much time. . . . So much time to think about yourself."

This wasn't simply a perfunctory expression of friendly jealousy. No, it was obvious from her tone that she truly felt that I had something she didn't. I wanted to tell her that she was wrong, that at least she had a husband, a house, a kid. But I couldn't bring myself to tell her how painful and terrifyingly lonely it was to have nothing but time to think only about myself. And even if I did tell her, to what end? I could sense that at some point, our lives had diverged and were now running parallel to each other's, separated by an ever-widening gap. Realizing what the future had in store for us, I could feel my heart start to sink inside my chest. Eventually, the gap between us would become too wide to cross, and all I could do was hope for some more time before that happened.

Before departing, Dabin left me with a few words.

"I wasn't going to mention this, but what the hell. Hyun-oh's back."

That night, I stayed up late tossing and turning. Dancing inside my head was that name. That name which I'd tried to forget, but which refused to be forgotten. Hyun-oh. As day broke, I was finally able to erase his name from my thoughts and get a couple of hours of sleep.

* * *

Mr. Nam's house wasn't far from the academy. I was walking along a street lined with shady bars when I came upon a low-rise multi-plex. As I walked toward it through the alleyway, I saw drunk men on the ground and women covered in thick makeup chewing gum. Not the best place to raise a child.

I rang the bell, and Mr. Nam opened the door to greet me in an outfit that looked like he'd just come back from a run. The apartment was small and poorly furnished. The color of the walls and the floor reminded me of over-scorched rice. And yet, despite its drab and cramped appearance, the whole apartment was filled with the nutty aroma of great cooking. Spread out on a low table in the living room were Vietnamese spring rolls and other finger food to accompany drinking. I sat down and started admiring a packed bookcase. Most were parenting books about connecting with teenage children.

"You're an unusually good cook," Muin said. He and Gyuok had arrived before me and they were already munching on something.

"A father's gotta protect his daughter from endocrine disruptors. Not a day goes by that I don't read some article that says they're tampering with our food. If there's one thing I know how to do, it's make my daughter a good meal. If you don't believe me, just look."

Mr. Nam dropped his gaze and sheepishly rubbed his large stomach. It turned out that Mr. Nam was currently working odd jobs and gigs he acquired through a contracting agency. In December, he played Santa Claus at department stores, and the rest of the time, he made visits to children's birthdays dressed up as a clown. He acknowledged that he wasn't the cutest old man in the world, but that he was popular with the kids nonetheless.

"Well, don't keep your talents to yourself and your daughter." Gyuok was slurping on a bowl of noodles. "You should make a food blog. With enough unique recipes and a good photographer, you might even be able to put out a book."

"Sounds like a hassle. Keeping a blog would require me to learn how to write, and I'm not diligent enough to take pictures of every meal." Mr. Nam picked up some noodles with his chopsticks before adding quietly, "Actually, there is something I'm working on. It's kind of embarrassing though."

We went back and forth for several minutes trying to get him to tell us what it was he was working on, but he refused to tell us his secret. And just as we were getting tipsy and about to give up, he looked at us with a face eager to talk.

"You *really* want to know?"

We'd already resigned ourselves to ignorance, but he paid no attention to our lukewarm reaction and sat the three of us in front of his computer.

"Don't think badly of me for this. After all, a man's gotta make money, right? Gosh, I don't think I can be in the room while you three watch. I'll stand over there. I wonder, is this what actors feel like when they see their face on the big screen?"

The three of us squeezed our heads around the frame of the monitor, like a brood of chicks pecking at the same pile of seeds. It was a video of Mr. Nam eating spaghetti. He was just eating without saying a word. After inhaling an entire plate of noodles and washing it down with a two-liter bottle of Coke, he moved on to dismembering a roasted chicken.

"What is this?" someone asked.

Mr. Nam scratched his head. "It's mukbang." Mukbang, an online broadcast in which someone consumes large quantities of food for viewers. Something I'd only ever heard about but never watched personally. Mr. Nam bragged about how he had relatively high viewership when compared to other mukbang streamers, as if it were something to be proud of.

"But why?"

"Loneliness, I guess."

The way he answered was as though he'd anticipated the question.

"I don't have a lot of opportunities to eat with others. When I stream, it feels like someone is watching over me. I can see people's comments in real time on the side of the screen. Of course, sometimes people say mean things about my weight, but most of the time, people in the chat are encouraging. They thank me for inspiring them. And that gives me a lot of strength."

Mr. Nam then started scrolling through a folder of recordings, saying he wanted to show us his most popular stream. What he eventually showed us was a video of him cooking, but not in the usual sense.

"I got the idea from a memory I had of cooking when my daughter was just a baby. This is back from when my channel was its most popular."

He was making porridge for babies with broccoli, spinach, and ground beef. But he wasn't just cooking baby food. He *was* a baby. He was dressed in a baby hat and a bib and even had red blush on his cheeks to make himself look cuter. And when he was done cooking, he gorged himself on the food, just like in the other video.

"Shit, I can't watch this."

No sooner did Muin say this than he apologized to Mr. Nam.

Mr. Nam turned off the screen looking embarrassed.

"I get it. Viewers pity me when I tell them I have a daughter."

"Do you like eating that much?"

"No. I told you. It's loneliness."

Mr. Nam then lowered his voice to a whisper.

"I wouldn't be doing this if my wife were still around. It all started one day when we were video chatting. We don't video chat much these days because of the time difference, but when she first moved abroad, I would videocall her every meal so that I didn't feel lonely. But after a while, she lost interest in watching me eat. She said that as long as I'm pooping well, she doesn't care what I stuff my face with. And how could I argue with that? But then I started uploading the videos online, and I got a lot of views. People even complimented me on my cooking. They told me to post more. I make a bit of side cash doing this, too."

Mr. Nam fell silent for a moment, as though thinking about something, before letting out a melancholic sigh.

"I've got lots of reasons for why I do it. But if there's anyone to blame, it's that asshole."

He lowered his voice.

"I used to be a cook. My specialty was tteokbokki. These days, there are a lot of tteokbokki chains. Hell, even buffets have it these days. But it wasn't more than ten years ago when the only place you could get it was street stalls. And *I* was one of the people who brought it into the restaurant. I spent a whole year of my life to make a killer recipe. All I ate was pepper sauce and rice cake. And I only stopped once I was satisfied. Then one day, this guy shows up at my store. He asks me if I want to enter a business partnership with him. He says he has his own store. So we shook on it. And in the beginning, it was great. That was the first time in my life I'd made so much money. But then he stole my recipe and opened his own chain. Do you wanna know who it was? It was this guy."

He took out an old magazine and threw it on the table. It was a food magazine from ten years ago. On the front cover was a thinner version of Mr. Nam with his arm around another man's shoulder.

"That's Han Yeong-cheol!" Muin blurted out.

There wasn't a person in Korea who didn't know that name. Heartthrob actor from the '90s turned trendy businessman and restaurant owner, he used his experience from appearing on cooking programs and the wealth inherited from his parents to put a store in every alley in Korea. This was the man Mr. Nam was posing with for a tteokbokki restaurant advertisement.

"It took a year to make that recipe. I ate tteokbokki every day, until my tongue went numb and my belly was as soft as rice cake. That's how I made that taste."

According to Mr. Nam, Han Yeong-cheol had tricked him into a false partnership. They were working together, but everything was in Han's name. Because of this, Mr. Nam had to pay royalties every time he used his own recipe. He called news channels and accused Han of intellectual theft and even put on a one-man protest outside one of his restaurants, but to no avail. In the end, he stepped away from the restaurant business, after which Han opened a new chain. Once he did that, Mr. Nam lost any chance to gain recognition for his efforts. It was as though he never existed.

Mr. Nam's monologue ended. The tears filling his eyes were so sincere that I knew he couldn't be making it up. He pressed his fingers into the floor, causing them to turn white.

"Why don't you do anything?" Gyuok asked quietly.

I could feel the air pushed by his voice grazing my shoulder.

"I did! I went on TV. I put on a one-man protest. I got a lawyer. But nothing changed. I did everything I could."

Han had entered politics in the last general election, winning a seat in the national assembly for one of the many conservative parties in Korea. But it wasn't just Han. The whole country had seen a slew of celebrities-turned-politicians under the name of reform for the business sector. But they were all just front men for their parties. They didn't really do anything of significance.

"Every night, I couldn't sleep. I was so mad at myself for not being able to get in his face and tell him off. If only I had confronted him when I had the chance, I don't think I would have so many regrets and feel so betrayed. Not a day goes by that I don't think about it. But I've completely lost all hope."

"Well, now's the time to give him a piece of your mind." It was Gyuok, speaking in code again. "To lose hope is to give up. And you should never give up. You're probably not the only one he's done this to. Han's used your food to delude people and to get onto TV shows. You think people are happier because of him? All he's done is use his fame to enter politics. His chain has put mom-and-pop shops out of business, and he's profited from other people's hard work. And now, he's receiving a paycheck from taxpayers every month while he sits on his ass all day. And I'm not suggesting that you take out your anger in secret. At the right time and right place, let's give him his just deserts. All within the confines of the law, of course. What we're doing is sending a warning to other people like Han. We're making an example of him. He should be honored that of all the lowlifes in the world"—Gyuok paused and reached into a bag of corn chips. He swirled his hand once before pulling out a single chip—"he was lucky enough to have been picked by us."

He dumped the remainder of the corn chips into his mouth and started munching on them. There was something symbolic in the way the sound of the chips crunching in his mouth sounded like the air itself was shattering.

A few days later, I looked up Mr. Nam's mukbang recordings. I had to go through a tedious process to see them. Not only did I have to make an account on a niche forum, but I also had to write a post introducing myself as someone who likes to "eat alone." When I finally gained member privileges, the website I found was, at the same time, both colorful and depressingly drab. Because I didn't know Mr. Nam's ID, I had to sift through hundreds of videos without any direction. People of all shapes and sizes were gorging themselves on all sorts of food. I saw mukbangs of a young boy in a school uniform, of a 220-pound self-proclaimed vegan eating only beans, asparagus, and bananas; of a personal trainer advertising the best diet to build muscle; of people eating pounds and pounds of jjajangmyeon or bread or cream cake. Watching these things, I couldn't help but pity them. I was just about to give up when I finally stumbled upon Mr. Nam's videos. His online alias pulled on my heartstrings. Dear Daddy.

I steadied my heart, which was already threatening to become heavy, and silently watched a playlist of his videos. Sometimes he would stare at the camera with wistful eyes, as though he were praying for someone to be watching, and sometimes he would sing or read the comments aloud. But always he was eating, and eating, and eating.

Questions, one after another, popped into my mind. I couldn't understand why anyone would film themselves for others to watch. Who started this trend? And why? Was it just a desperate plea for attention, a need to feel acknowledged in every aspect of life? Where would people draw the line? And just as puzzling as the people who made these videos were the people who watched them. Who watched videos like this? I thought about the phrase "putting food on the table." Why did people use that phrase so often? Did people eat to work, or work to eat? Only after I realized that something warm was running down my cheek did I finally close the window in shock. I didn't like this. Shedding tears for someone you couldn't do anything for. I suppressed my anger as I dabbed the moisture from my face.

I hopped on Han Yeong-cheol's home page. It was your typical congressperson's home page, filled with personal achievements and career highlights designed to self-promote. He also had many pictures with "commoner people," as if to say he was one of us. But I knew that behind that facade, he was enjoying privileges at the expense of other people. I became sad for Mr. Nam as I watched Han smile and take a bite of fish cake, a common ingredient in tteokbokki. But I focused my emotions. There were times to be sad and times to be angry. And right now, I needed to be angry.

10

THE FIRST COUNTERATTACK

A few days later, the four of us were at a traditional market located in Han Yeong-cheol's district eating bowls of hot noodles. The market had once been a bustling tourist attraction but had slowly been dying for some time now because of the large supermarket across the street. In fact, one of the reasons that Han had been elected was because of his promise to save the local traditional market, a pledge he backed up with his history as a restaurant owner. From the looks of it, he'd done little to uphold that promise. I couldn't help but feel a little depressed looking at this half-abandoned market and the few mom-and-pop shops that were just barely managing to survive.

The restaurant we were eating at distinguished itself from other shops with its large bowls of anchovy broth, giant servings of slightly undercooked noodles that remained al dente all the way to the last bite, and generous amounts of tasty garnishing to bring out the flavor and color. It was a good thing too, because had the serving sizes been any smaller, we might have been upset when the middle-aged owner threw the bowls onto the table and spilled broth everywhere. In fact, there was still a half bowl of noodles sitting in front of me when I'd already eaten what would normally have been one full serving. I lifted my head for a breather when I heard someone chuckling in front of me.

"I sometimes eat with glasses, too, so I get it. But you looked just like Arale from *Dr. Slump.*"

Gyuok continued to laugh at me with his arms crossed. I buried my head in the bowl of noodles instead of replying to him. Everyone had that one thing they just couldn't do. For some it was swimming, others, whistling. As for me, the one thing I could never hope to do was eat noodles while enjoying a TV program. Either my glasses would get too foggy to see the screen, or my vision would be too blurry to make out the people. Damned if you do, damned if you don't. The only option I had if I ever wanted to enjoy a TV dinner was to get contacts or LASIK. But as it was, neither of those appealed to me.

When we finished eating, we went over our plan one step at a time. According to his official home page, Congressman Han (that was his new official title) would be making a visit to the market today around 4 p.m. It was an outing he made regularly to keep up approval ratings in his district. Even so, he remained unpopular among store owners because he hadn't stopped the large supermarket across the street from growing even larger. Everyone here knew all too well that he'd failed to deliver on the promises that got him into office. And while it seemed like he wasn't too bothered by their disapproval of him, it was just enough to make him take an occasional lap around the market to get photo ops with shop owners and show the voters that he was connecting with the "average Korean."

According to our sources, Han would be accompanied by half a dozen aides as he marched through the market, only stopping once for photos in front of a traditional Korean snacks store, which un-coincidentally was the best-looking shop in the whole market. We trusted this information because one of his aides had already visited the store to set up the photo op. Anyway, when Han arrived at the store, I was to approach him and get his attention. Gyuok would be in position to take photos when Mr. Nam and Muin threw eggs at him.

I had a disguise on to make myself look like the most inconspic-uously average woman I could. So naturally, all I had to do was put on a bit of makeup and dress like an office worker. It didn't take much to turn me into a woman that none of my friends or family would recognize. As I reapplied a generous layer of powder to my face, Muin was getting into an argument with Mr. Nam, who had just declared he wanted to call it quits.

"You can't back out now. I've wasted an entire day of writing just to come here. I just cured my writer's block. Do you know how hard it was sacrificing an entire day of writing to come here?"

"I just can't do it. What if I go to jail? What will happen to Ji-yool? It'll be easy to establish a motive. They might even give me a harsher sentence because it's premeditated. If I'm gone, Jiyool might as well call herself an orphan."

"Han is a congressman. I doubt he's going to press charges on a civilian just because of a few eggs. His position won't allow him to stoop to our level."

Gyuok didn't say anything as Muin and Mr. Nam went back and forth like this without progress. And now, the restaurant owner was starting to give us dirty looks, like we were obnoxious patrons staying past closing.

Gyuok finally spoke up. "Let's call it quits if you can't do it." His tone was cold, but his facial expression was a smile filled with compassionate pity. "No one knows what will happen if we go through with this. But it's your decision, Mr. Nam. You're the one who will be most affected by this. If you're satisfied getting paid to eat on film for strangers, then we should call it quits and go home. You'll have to live with the regret, but maybe you can just scream into your pillow when you feel like it."

Gyuok's somewhat irritated manner of speaking made it hard for anyone to respond.

"Fine, I'll do it," Mr. Nam finally said. "You're right."

Mr. Nam boldly slapped two 10,000-won bills on the table as though this were his last meal and marched out of the restaurant.

Each of us found a hiding spot near the store and waited for the man of the hour. Congressman Han and his associates appeared in the distance, bringing with them a wake of low commotion. A few shop owners surrounded him and began clapping. My palms became sweaty as I waited for him to walk to the spot. There was a slight hiccup when one of the ladies of the market refused to shake Han's hand and started demanding an explanation for why he hadn't saved the market like he promised. After his political aides successfully ushered her out of the way, Han twisted his frown back into a smile again and continued his pilgrimage through the market. Eventually, he arrived outside the traditional Korean snacks store.

Now that I had a good look at him, he was shorter and oilier than I imagined. A face speckled with liver spots and a back so hunched that it resisted his best efforts to walk upright—he was your typical sixty-year-old man, and a shadow of that TV star from the '90s. If it weren't for his nice suit and the golden badge on his chest, I doubt I'd ever give him the time of day. I had assumed that he would have an imposing aura because of all his fame, but he gave me no such feeling.

He greeted the owner of the shop and said a few kind words. Now was our chance. Gyuok pushed me from behind. The firmness of it surprised me. With the momentum he imparted to me, I was immediately thrust to the front of the crowd, just feet away from Han.

"Congressman. I'm a huge fan. I have a present for you. Please, try some."

I smiled and offered him a piece of sticky yeot. It might not have seemed like much, but it was very expensive as far as stage props went. I'd bought it from the shop earlier. It was handmade and the most expensive the store had to offer. Han looked a bit weary, but with so many people watching, he had no choice but to accept the gift. Just as he bit off a piece of the yeot, someone shouted at us.

"Congressman. That's a great picture. Look this way."

It was Gyuok. I used this as my opportunity to slip back into the crowd. My role had ended. As soon as I was out of harm's way, eggs started raining down on Han's head. One after another, after another. Unable to process what was happening, Han was still smiling for the camera with a piece of yeot in his mouth as the yolk, which was as yellow as spring forsythia, dripped from his hair.

"Eat yeot!" It was Muin's voice. "And don't forget the eggs!"

Immediately, Gyuok's camera shutter went off like a machine gun loaded with bolts of lightning. In the distance, I heard Mr. Nam scream out like a crazed man.

"What a waste of eggs. He's just a charlatan that steals other people's recipes. He's worse than shit!"

* * *

"But the eggs were fertilized, I'm telling you. That was all they had at the store. I feel so guilty. Those poor unborn chicks."

Mr. Nam really sounded like he felt bad for the chickens, but he still could not hold back the glee in his voice.

"It's okay. Even if they had been born, they would have been kept in small cages at a chicken farm and force-fed for slaughter. And then they'd be like this—"

Muin stopped and took a bite of a fried chicken leg. I couldn't tell if what he said was touching or simply depressing. We toasted with our beer cans, and as they touched, they let out a dull sound.

After the prank, we rendezvoused at Muin's place. As you'd expect from an aspiring writer, his bookcase was filled with books about writing screenplays and novels. Every thirty seconds, Mr. Nam checked the phone in his hand and giggled to himself. Filling his screen was a picture of Han covered in yolk and taking a bite of yeot. The picture was well taken and aided by the high contrast from the afternoon sun. In fact, the quality of the photo and the way Han smiled joyfully as yellow goo dripped from his forehead, made it look like a professionally designed movie poster for a comedy. Mr. Nam had no intention of making the photo public. It was literally just a commemorative photograph, a picture taken to remember what he'd accomplished today.

"I guess I'm not the only one who hates him. Did you hear what the store owners said when we egged him? 'Throw more! Another, another!'"

"You're a good shot. I missed all three of my eggs, but you hit all of yours."

Muin's compliments seemed to embolden Mr. Nam.

"I might not look like it, but I wanted to be a professional baseball player when I was a kid. Back when they still called it *primary school.*"

Mr. Nam retold the heroic tale from his point of view, and each time he told it, he added new things that hadn't been there before.

"Of course, you were amazing!"

The way Muin praised Mr. Nam made it seem like he was passing the mantle from himself as a calligraphy graffiti artist to Mr. Nam as an egg-wielding political assassin.

"Thank you. I wouldn't have been able to do it if it weren't for you three."

Mr. Nam gently dabbed the perspiration on his forehead. Even if his daughter didn't know about what happened today, in my eyes at least, he was a superdad. And I would have told him this too, had I the courage to do so.

"You guys don't think I'll be arrested, do you?"

Mr. Nam had asked this question more than twenty times already.

"Are you kidding me?" Gyuok laughed. "I bet there's a manhunt for you as we speak. They'll have handcuffs on you in no time."

And yet, all of us became nervous as the eight o'clock news drew near. I feigned confidence that we'd be safe, but secretly my heart was pounding with fear that someone had taken a picture of me at the market. But in the end, a small incident at a dying traditional market was too insignificant to become big news, especially with everything going on in the world at the time. There were more shocking and sensational things to report on. We flipped through the various news channels for a while, and once we realized we were in the clear, we all cheered. Soon, Muin's small studio apartment became filled with the sound of laughter and toasting. There was, however, one person who posted on Twitter about what happened at the market.

> OMG! Some guy just egged @congressmanhanyeongcheol! I hope they show it on the news.

But the person didn't have a picture it seemed. Nor was the post retweeted, probably because the person didn't have many followers. But this amount of recognition was more than enough for Mr. Nam, who called the fried chicken restaurant and ordered another chicken and beer to celebrate.

Despite not making the news that night, we were anxious for several days that the police might get involved. But it seemed that Han had no intention of finding the culprits. After all, what we'd done was a relatively harmless prank. Mr. Nam kept the picture from that day as the wallpaper on his cell phone.

"It's a shame that no one else is going to see it. As long as it's not going public, I might as well look at it as often as I can. And for some reason, looking at pictures of people eating yeot makes me happy. I think I'll take a short break from doing mukbangs."

I was happy that Mr. Nam was pleased with the results, even though I knew that what we'd done was risky. But I was having fun, too. At least until my mind became preoccupied with other matters.

11

ANTITHESIS

Noona, what are you up to these days?"

This was the question Jihwan asked me as we ate dinner the night he showed up on my doorstep with a large suitcase in his hand.

"What do ya think? Eating, working, and looking for a better job. Don't tell Mom and Dad that I'm living in a semi-basement apartment, okay?"

I raised one eyebrow menacingly.

"Fine. I just asked because I was worried you were studying again," Jihwan mumbled as he pointed to the stack of books on the linoleum floor. "If not, whatever."

"I borrowed them from the academy to prepare lecture materials. And besides, reading and getting a liberal arts education is important, no matter what work you end up doing."

"Sure it is."

I wanted to tell him I didn't like his attitude, but then stopped myself. He was planning to stay here for two weeks, and I wanted to remain cordial for as long as possible. Suddenly, he stabbed the doenjang-jjigae with his spoon.

"Noona, do you still think I'm uneducated? You're always going on about liberal arts this, liberal arts that. It pisses me off."

My voice felt small when I replied, "I've never said I think you're uneducated."

Jihwan was a good kid—at least when he wasn't acting up. He hadn't gone to college, a decision of his own that no one tried to oppose. Instead, after graduating from a technical high school, he found work at an auto shop and worked there for a while before switching to sales. At his current job, he got good performance evaluations, was paid well, and had a clear career path. Given his thriftiness, it was no surprise when he moved from Seoul down to Wonju to save money. In many ways, he was more decisive and proactive than I was—not to mention more successful. As far as I saw it, he was more than educated enough, and he was one of the few people of our generation who knew what they wanted to do with their lives. And yet, for some reason, he often demonstrated the signs of an inferiority complex, despite no one in our family having ever expressed disappointment in his not going to college. It seemed like today he was experiencing yet another flare-up of insecurity.

"I don't even know what *liberal arts* is. It's just one of those phrases that people throw around when they want to show off and put others down. But you know what? I heard eight out of ten people who graduate with a liberal arts degree can't get work. It just goes to show, humanities majors are useless out in the real world. Just like you, Noona."

"Hey!"

My hand balled into a fist on its own.

"Sorry. But you've got to face the truth. I stopped by a bookstore at the bus terminal today because I wanted something to read on the ride up to Seoul. There was so much 'literature' there. I opened one of them just to see what all the hoopla was about. I couldn't understand a single fucking word. Anyway, they offer a lot of liberal arts courses where you work, right?"

"Well, at least you're taking an interest in what I do for a living."

"I think it's all for show. English and philosophy majors might seem sexy in college or on TV, but society doesn't want them. They talk about it on the news every day. They say college students these days don't check out books from the library anymore. And after paying all that tuition! They say kids are too busy building up their resume and studying to get certificates. It's all about getting a job. So, then why are people always going on about how important the liberal arts are?"

Jihwan wasn't totally wrong. But what really bothered me wasn't his disdain for the humanities but rather the feeling of resentful inferiority that I knew lay at the heart of that disdain. I tried to gently respond to him.

"That's why you should find the time to take a course or two."

"No—" Jihwan said defiantly. "It's all vanity. Vanity for people with the time and money to waste on learning useless things. People run themselves into the ground studying to get certificates and raise their English test scores. But in the end, when you get into a company, what's really important is people. Even if all you're doing is peddling on the street, you still need to know how people think. That way you know how to set up the stand, what items to put on display, which things to sell to whom and why. You need to know people, and you need to know how the world works. But people are too embarrassed to read self-help books. So they go looking for something else to talk about at least. And what they find are liberal arts books. It's ironic that another word for liberal arts is the humanities. It's all about people in the end. I blame it all on Steve Jobs. He tried to put his soul into a machine, and he kind of succeeded. But is that possible in South Korea? And yet, because Koreans have such a talent for following trends, losers are flocking to bookshops and academies to become more cultured. What do you think?"

"I think you're onto something."

I needed to agree with him if I wanted to avoid hearing what was really brooding beneath the surface of these comments. But it was no use, because Jihwan said what he wanted to say anyway.

"I'm saying this because Mom and Dad won't, so listen up. I don't know what your plans are, but I think you should stop turning your nose up at the world and wake up. That's the best advice I can give you as a successful salesman. I might not know much about school, but I know this much. Isn't that impressive?"

He was saying this as if it were the conclusion to his previous comments. But to me, these words felt more like the body of his argument.

Jihwan unstuck his spoon from the stew and pulled out a piece of tofu. I wanted to give my rebuttal, but I didn't know where to start. The frustration was making my body tight, but why was I so frustrated? Jihwan studied my face for a moment before changing the subject.

"Anyway, do you have any vitamin C? They say it's good to start taking it before the surgery."

I opened and slammed several drawers looking for the vitamin C that I knew I had somewhere. Jihwan had come up to Seoul to get a LASIK procedure.

"You should get LASIK, too, if you want. It's cheap if you do a group buy."

"You can do group buys for LASIK?"

"It's Korea. You really don't think they'd do LASIK group buys? People send live puppies through the fucking mail. Hell, people even try to return puppies via the post, even though it's technically illegal. Anyways, *yes*, you can buy LASIK through group buys. You could probably make a business out of anything communal in Korea, even death."

"Is the surgery done as a group, too?"

Jihwan looked at me as if he thought me pathetically ignorant.

"No. As long as you pay the broker, they'll find enough heads to fill the MOQ. That's why it's so cheap. I don't even know who my surgeon is. It was the coordinator who gave me my consultation and exam. I won't see the doctor until it's time to get cut open. And after the procedure's done, I bet I'll never see him again. They have group buys for plastic surgery, too. I bet it works the same."

"Are you sure that's safe? I mean, we are talking about your eyes, after all."

"Everyone says that. Most people come out just fine. I doubt people would do it if it wasn't safe. You can't waste money, even on things like this."

I'd heard enough to know the reason why my body felt so tight with frustration.

"And what are you going to do with all the money you save?"

Jihwan looked at me in disbelief.

"Do I even need to say? I'm going to use that money to become rich and live a life of luxury. My goals in life used to be money, a house, a car, marriage, and lots of kids. But now I think I can do without the last two. I'd rather travel the world and spend money on my hobbies. All after I become a millionaire, of course."

I finally found the bottle of vitamin C supplements and tossed them on the table in front of him before going to my room. "Hey, these are expired!" he called out to me in dissatisfaction. But I ignored him and slammed the door. I couldn't believe that little twerp was going to spend an entire two weeks with me. Sometimes, it felt like family you hadn't seen in forever were more difficult to get along with than complete strangers. How had I survived nearly twenty years under the same roof with him?

Awhile later, Jihwan knocked on my door, but only once. He came into my room before I could give him permission to do so. He went straight over to my vanity and opened a lid of hair wax. I asked him what he was doing, and he said he'd just made plans to meet up with a girl he met on the forum for the LASIK group buy. How could two siblings be so different? I stared quietly at his reflection in the mirror. He leaned forward toward the glass and then ran both hands through his hair as though he were doing an Elvis impersonation.

"We were always complete opposites," he said as if reading my mind, his fingers still trying to work the wax through into his scalp. "And the older we get, the more different we become. You want an example? In the past, my first question on a date used to be whether she had fake tits or not. Now I just want to know what kind of car she drives. I guess that means I'm finally growing up. Unlike some people."

"Oh, fuck off!"

I threw my pillow at him. He could have dodged it, but instead he let it hit him as he smirked at me.

"I wanna be rich, Noona. Why? Cause it's the only way I can kick back and relax. It's not just for me. It's for everyone. You. Mom. Dad. Even my girlfriend—or wife if I'm lucky."

"Don't worry about me. And make all the money you want. I'm sure your future partner will like spending time with you more if you have money."

"You only think that way because you've never experienced generational wealth. Grow up, sis."

Jihwan threw the pillow back at me, and I dodged it. He was becoming a workaholic, just like our dad. But our father didn't work all the time because he liked it. He was just an average patriarch living in a time when men were expected to go out and make money while the women stayed home and took care of the children. That was why he spent more than half of his life sitting in the driver's seat of a taxicab. In his mind, the best way to express love for his struggling family was to bring home regular monthly paychecks. Accordingly, he wasted the best years of our childhood not knowing what it meant to spend time with family.

But he was one of the lucky ones. With all the money he'd made, he was able to buy the strawberry farm he'd always promised my mother. But now that I thought about it, there was something surreal about saving up money from driving taxicabs to buy a strawberry farm. It sounded more like something from a children's story. Things like that just weren't possible anymore.

In fact, I said this exact thing to him once, that life was different back then, and he snapped back at me, "Don't talk about what you haven't experienced." But perhaps that was just how our generations understood and saw each other. We each claimed that we had it harder and thought dismissively of the other generation, always staying away from each other like parallel lines. In that sense, perhaps having it hard and suffering was as much a fact of life back then as it was now. Regardless, he was now enjoying a modest life down in rural Wonju with my mother. In fact, I would say that he had a relatively successful retirement, even if he was always complaining about his knee pain and that we never called.

But when had Jihwan changed? There had been an incident not long after Jihwan graduated from high school. He had taken his guitar and ran to the house of his girlfriend who'd just asked for a breakup. He sat on the concrete and filled the alley with love songs so out of tune you'd think he was singing "Happy Birthday." He didn't give up, even when she refused to come out to talk with him, and only sang louder, until every alley in the neighborhood echoed with his maudlin song. "I'll die if it's not you. It's you and only you." It was I and not my parents who went to pick him up from the police station. I can still remember the way he rested his flushed face on my shoulder. He could barely catch his breath, and yet was stubbornly trying to say something to me. "Noona, I believe in love. Love is the most precious thing in the world. Did you know? We were born to love. I'll never give up on love. Love will save me . . ." I didn't think he knew what he was talking about, but I just sat there in silence and stroked his hair. Thinking about this, I couldn't help but feel a bit resentful toward the world for stealing my little brother's innocence.

Jihwan's surgery was a success, and after spending ten days recovering at my apartment, he returned to Wonju. He and the girl he'd met on that group-buy forum had dated for several days until Jihwan's vision returned, better than ever. After that, he completely lost interest in her. He said something about her being prettier before, that once he could see the pores on her face, he felt disillusioned. On the day he left, I could feel myself missing him already. Family was like that sometimes. You fought when you were together, but as soon as you were apart, you started missing each other. I tried to get him to let me go with him to the station, but he continued to refuse me.

"I like it cut and dry. No drawn-out goodbyes."

The little punk pushed me back through the front door and closed it on my face. The sound of his footsteps, neither heavy nor light, disappeared in a matter of seconds. I wiped his glasses, which he'd asked me to throw away for him, and placed them neatly on my desk. He'd just gotten LASIK, but I realized he'd already possessed a candid view of the world for some time now. I'd read once that dragonflies have thirty thousand eyes on each side of their head. How miserable must the world look through those eyes. Seeing the pores on his girlfriend's face had broken the illusion of love; I wasn't thrilled about what other cold truths Jihwan would be able to see now with his new eyes.

* * *

On Wednesday evenings after ukulele class, the four of us would migrate to the bar and conspire together on new pranks. We planned at the outset to avoid social media and the internet. Instigation via the internet was too common, too ineffective, too forgettable, too traceable. What we wanted was something totally original yet under the radar and hard to eradicate.

We started with a pastor who'd used church donations to make his family rich, and disrupted his service by banging on wooden

Buddhist moktaks and chanting "Namu Amita Bul, Namu Amita Bul." Then we made a scene at a trendy restaurant that was infamous for refusing service to disabled people by dressing up as bums and waving cash in their face. We even waited outside a supermarket for a manager who was withholding pay from employees, dancing and cheering with masks that read, "Pay Your Workers!"

Our targets were people who abused their authority and made the world a worse place. Our mission was to make them feel uncomfortable and ashamed, to show them they were wrong. The reaction was always the same: shocked and bewildered, as though a bucket of cold water had just washed away the mistaken belief that they were hydrophobic to shame's constant drizzle. I could almost hear them cursing under their breath:

Do you know who I am? How dare you. Who do you think you are?

What do you think you're accomplishing by doing this?

Our weekly counterattacks straddled the line between acceptable and unacceptable risk. If we were caught, they were too harmless to get more than a slap on the wrist, and too short and intimate to risk being sued for defamation. Just like the prank we played on Han, there was enough cause for our victims to press charges, but we were counting on their desire to save face and not draw further attention to their own moral failings. It was exhilarating, brainstorming together and putting our plans into action. We felt alive, like we had the key to the city. And every week, we celebrated our success with a simple toast in secret.

Reports of and reactions to our pranks were posted online and even made it to the pages of a few small magazines. The reception was generally positive, and the public wanted to know our identity. Some categorized our pranks as a political performance or a new type of performance art. We even had a few copycats.

Most important, we'd brought individual wrongdoings out into the public again for discussion. At the same time, we made sure to select our targets carefully and only do pranks that were short and metaphorical, nothing that would garner us too much attention.

But it was this fact that started to bother me. Even though our pranks were successful and gratifying, it still felt like we were dancing around the true target, never hitting a bull's-eye. But I never let these doubts escape my lips. Our meetings were like a social club to me, one of my only ways to communicate with the rest of the world. And because of that, I needed to play it safe. I didn't have the courage to take greater action anyway, and it wasn't my dream to sacrifice myself to save the world. It was for this reason that I was adrift. Aside from any personal interest I might have in Gyuok, I never thought of myself as one of them. I knew it was horrible of me, but somewhere deep in my heart, I considered myself a temporary guest, someone who was just passing through, someone who would soon be forgotten. Eventually, I wanted to leave them and come up in the world. I avoided guilt by convincing myself that they must all be thinking the same way. Whenever I felt a sense of kinship and comfort around them, I wanted to escape the most.

One day, I called into the office sick. But instead of staying home, I went to interview for a position at the culture planning division of a midsize company. I'd already passed the document screening phase and made it to the final interview. I'd sent in my resume without great expectations, but when I learned that I was just one of two finalists, I couldn't help but wonder, *What if?*

The company had what looked like a bright future as it had recently cashed in on several investments in the movie industry. As I answered the well-dressed interviewers' questions, I began to envision myself working there. Scanning my employee card at the elevator. Opening my laptop at a Starbucks to work during weekends. Going to movie premieres and art exhibitions on weekday afternoons. Visiting large bookstores to peruse the New Releases section for books that might make good movies. I know that I usually whine about doing extra work, but this seemed positively luxurious compared to the soul-sucking copying and errand running I did at Diamant.

I gave them the best version of myself. I told a believable white lie that I was making important contributions to the planning division at Diamant Academy, a subsidiary of DM, and presented myself as a refined and cultured person. And when they asked me if I would be willing to work late or on weekends for important deadlines, I mustered all the fibers in my neck to nod my head. "Of course!" Despite all my talk of minimal labor, I was still willing to sacrifice evenings and weekends if it meant I could make a proper place for myself in the world.

Deep down, however, the antithetical propositions from Jihwan and Gyuok were colliding in my mind and torturing me. Jihwan told me to wise up and accept reality, and Gyuok said I needed the courage to reject and break it. But there was one point of overlap between these two propositions: both terrified me.

12

ELDERLY CITIZEN

They said they would reach out to the winning candidate, but it'd already been four days since the interview and my phone still hadn't rung. My memory of the interviewers' friendly smiles was already starting to fade. There had only been one other candidate, and I could tell from my vantage point that she had mumbled her answers in a quiet and halting voice, her body language drooping and lacking conviction. There was absolutely no way I would lose in a one-on-one competition with her. There had to be a mistake. Either they were postponing their decision because someone was sick, or they'd lost my phone number because of some freak accident and were running around with their hair on fire trying to figure out what to do.

Just before lunch, I went out into the hallway and worked up the courage to call them. I navigated my way through their maze-like automated caller system, before finally getting in contact with the person in charge of hires. Her voice was friendly. I asked if they'd made their decision. "Yes." I asked if they'd contacted the hire. "We have." "All right. I understand." My voice sounded up-beat, almost like I was thanking them for rejecting me.

I walked back to my desk. Team Leader Yu offered to take me out for lunch. Sushi, she said. But I didn't have the strength to eat lunch with her right now while acting like nothing was wrong. My usual excuse came flying out of my mouth.

"I'm having lunch with Jeong-jin."

I walked through the park inside the apartment complex. I could see several people exercising in the open air. They trained their muscles, pulling and pushing on iron bars, and ran around the track until they were out of breath and sunburned. These people were making the most of their lives. I felt a pain in my chest. I would never arrive at tomorrow. I would never escape from today like I wanted to. I was stuck. Around and around a track I'd go until eventually I collapsed from exhaustion.

I was walking absent-mindedly around the track when people started to yell at me. "You're going the wrong way! Watch where you're going!" An elderly woman dressed in a tracksuit glared at me as she power walked in the opposite direction. I looked around and realized that I was the only one walking the wrong way. Even here, on this small track in a park, there was a direction I should have been following but wasn't. I'd become a thoughtless person who goes against the flow of traffic, ruining things for everyone else.

I sat on a bench, dropped my head, and placed my palms to the left and right of my legs. The rough, old wood dug into the skin of my fingertips. And just as tears started to form in my eyes, a large shadow cast itself across my face.

"He's not real, is he?"

I lifted my head to discover Gyuok standing in front of me. He was smiling at me, but I didn't like his smile for some reason.

"Did you follow me here?" My voice sounded irritable.

"I guess you could say that. I just wanted to see his face. The first time, I thought he stood you up. The second time I wondered if he was invisible. And the third time, I just realized he wasn't real. Mr. Jeong-jin, I mean."

I was speechless and my face was turning red. I couldn't believe I'd been caught. No, I couldn't believe he'd been following me. My embarrassment almost outweighed my resentment, but not quite.

"He's real to me. And I need him."

"Why do you need him?"

"Why is everyone—" My voice was becoming shrill. Frustration surged through my veins. "Why is everyone so selfish? Sometimes, a person just wants to be left alone. Why can't you people just let me be? And you wonder why I invented an invisible man?"

Gyuok stood there in silence for a moment before responding. "I guess only someone like Mr. Jeong-jin would be good company to someone who wants to be left alone. I'll let you be. Wasn't trying to bother you."

And yet, instead of leaving, he sat down next to me, took out a pair of earbuds, and inserted them into my ears. I could hear the dissonant plucking of a few piano keys and then the sweet and slightly nasally voice of a man. The voice belonged to Harry Connick Jr. "Don't Get Around Much Anymore." The faint mellow melody filled my ears. Birds, joggers—never had they looked more like extras in a movie, set props just for me.

The wind caressed my face and scattered a few petals across the ground. The sky was pastel blue, and the ground was dyed light pink. I didn't recall the cherry blossoms ever blooming this year, but now petals from the sky were floating to the ground on the backs of gentle zephyrs. Without my knowledge, time had already slipped into mid-April. The slow swing of Gyuok's music, with its emphasis on the offbeat, gradually soothed my rapid heartbeat.

The music ended and Gyuok stood up. He took a few steps before turning around.

"But why the name Jeong-jin? Ex-boyfriend? Or—"

I just shrugged my shoulders without answering. Gyuok raised his hands as if to say, "Fine." As I watched him disappear into the distance, a mysterious feeling of relief washed over me. A tiny pocket of warmth bloomed in the tips of my fingers and spread to the rest of my body. And with this sudden wave of warmth, my body rustled like a tree in spring, as if to chase away the cold.

Perhaps this had been what I was hoping for every time I met Mr. Jeong-jin. Someone to tell me that Mr. Jeong-jin didn't exist. Someone to tell me I shouldn't be alone. Someone to sit with me in silence. Someone who extends their hand and offers to chase away the cold loneliness.

Spring semester was coming to an end, which meant that the ukulele class would soon be over. The class would, however, continue into the summer semester as Beginning Ukulele 2, and it seemed like everyone aside from the mother with her two children, who'd dropped the class, would be moving up to the next level.

Out of all the students, it was the son of the depressed mother who showed the most promise. And because he was the most talented, the instructor focused all of his attention on the young boy, leaving the rest of us struggling to keep up. Sometimes, he would even show the class videos of Jake Shimabukuro and other Hawaiian ukulele prodigies, in hopes that this young boy might become his star pupil someday. The boy's mother, who was aware enough to see that her son was getting preferential treatment, always apologized to the other students and would sometimes bake cookies or bread for the class. Muin and Mr. Nam were content to take this edible form of apology and continue plucking away at their instruments without guidance. I personally thought the instructor's conduct was unprofessional, but as an employee of the academy, I had no choice but to keep quiet.

The classroom was still drafty, despite it being late spring, and the four of us never talked or exchanged looks in class, as if we had a tacit agreement to act like complete strangers at the academy. We held our instruments up to our ears as we competed against the noise. And then one day while doing just this, a thought occurred to me. Perhaps that's life: plucking away at a four-stringed instrument by yourself and making soft yet crude sounds while competing against others doing the exact same thing, all in a vain attempt to hear just a whisper of your own voice.

* * *

It was Friday morning when I received a message from Dept. Head Kim. He asked me to meet him at a café for lunch, and to tell no one. My body went stiff as soon as I read this message. Recently, he'd become noticeably reclusive. Ever since the incident with the letter, he seemed out of place in the office, as though he'd become an entirely different person. In fact, he hadn't been to the office for the past two days. But why did he want to see *me*?

I arrived at the café and was glancing around when suddenly he appeared before me. His hair was mussed like a youth who'd been trying unsuccessfully for years to pass the civil service exam, and the porous skin on his face seemed to be losing a battle against gravity.

This was my first time having lunch alone with him. He was in his fifties as far as I knew, but now that he sat in front of me, he looked to be at least a decade older than that. His messy hair was lusterless and beginning to gray at the sideburns, and I could see large dandruff flakes embedded in his hairline like a crystalline structure. I had to scoot back in my chair whenever he scratched his head, but just slowly enough not to offend him. He talked about the weather for a moment before suddenly jumping to the point.

"You're the first person I'm telling this to. I won't be here starting next week. I just wanted to thank you for all your hard work."

My jaw dropped. Dept. Head Kim was quitting? The word "shocking" wasn't enough to describe how unexpectedly sudden this was. He was stubbornly antidemocratic, of course, and had bad table manners, but no one could deny that he was the one who made the academy what it was. Putting the academy on the map with good courses, convincing minicelebrities to come teach here, ensuring we had a steady stream of students and new registries—all of this was what he'd accomplished for the company.

"The others don't know yet. I've already handed in my letter of resignation to the top. I'm going to come in on the weekend to collect my stuff, when no one's around."

He let out a long sigh. My body was shaking against my will.

"It's not because of that note, is it?" I asked.

Dept. Head Kim wore a faint smile.

"No. Got nothing to do with that. Of course, I've never been the same after what happened."

This weak reassurance didn't comfort me.

"I only *say* letter of resignation. The truth of the matter is, I was fired. But they wanted me to be the one to resign, to save face. I guess it was my time. For a while now, I've felt like a terminally ill patient clinging onto his life support machine."

I'd heard rumors that once upon a time, Dept. Head Kim had been a hotshot at HQ before suddenly being transferred to the academy. When I first heard, I had a hunch that his transfer hadn't been completely voluntary, just like the resignation he'd just told me about wasn't. But I'd never imagined that one day, I'd learn the real reason he came to the academy—and straight from the horse's mouth, too.

It turned out that Dept. Head Kim had been slowly working his way up the ranks at the food marketing division at HQ. But then, just as they were about to release a new product, a competitor beat them to the punch with an identical product. There were all sorts of theories about what had happened. Most likely someone junior had betrayed the company and leaked the information to the competitor. Either way, Kim was in charge, so he had to take the fall.

"When I came into the office the next day, my desk was out in the hallway. But I just put my head down and worked as if nothing had changed. All day every day, for an entire month. And each day I went to my colleague and begged him to let me stay. He'd entered the company the same time as me, but there I was, on my knees begging *him* to keep me. I agreed to be transferred here and just barely avoided getting axed."

Dept. Head Kim looked like he was getting worked up telling this story. He paused and let out a deep sigh.

"Anyway, I did my best. I worked myself to the bone and used every trick in the book because I wasn't going to accept defeat. It was a dirty and shameful game. The kind of game where the harder you try to win, the closer you get to defeat. The kind of game that punishes honest struggles. I put up a good fight, everything considered."

"But why now?" I asked in a daze.

"I scored poorly on my performance evaluation. It's funny. Working hard and being on someone's good side don't always go hand in hand. You've gotta have self-awareness, and I've got none. I don't know who wrote that note, but I'm positive that Team Leader Yu mentioned it to HQ. They probably interpreted it as a sign that I wasn't getting along with other employees. And it was reflected in my performance evaluation. But you know what's even funnier? I don't even care who wrote the note, nor do I want to do anything to uncover their identity."

As I listened, I picked at the callus on my finger underneath the table. When I asked him what he was going to do now, he turned to look out the window.

"The only thing an old unemployed man like me *can* do. Self-employment. Start a business or something. Most people take that route. Or maybe I'll become a regular at reemployment job fairs. Who knows? We might run into each other again at my new fried chicken business. I'll make sure to give you a good discount."

He laughed bitterly when he mentioned the prospect of himself running a chicken restaurant.

"Anyway, I wanted to thank you. You were honest and always a diligent worker. No one can deny that. That's why I put in a recommendation for you. Better one of our own than a new person. You've still got passion."

My chest tightened at the word "passion."

"I wanted to do something good for the world before I left. Or perhaps I just wanted to cleanse my bad karma. That's why I called you out here before I left. Congratulations, Jihye! You're going to be a regular employee now."

The suddenness of this news left me bewildered. I was too shocked to say anything and felt too icky to be happy. Dept. Head Kim seemed to have already read the look on my face.

"You don't need to feel bad. I wasn't always like this, you know. Back in the '80s, back when your generation was born, I was one of the protestors who took to the streets and fought for our democracy. I screamed for change, for something to be done about the direction the world was headed. Shouted for our right to vote for our own president. Denounced the government for torturing that student to death. We lay on the street and sang until we couldn't sing anymore. I didn't care what happened to me. Back then, changing the world was more important."

Dept. Head Kim's mouth quivered slightly. There were deep creases to the left and right of his mouth, like a pair of parentheses.

Lunchtime was almost over. He pulled himself together and got up from his seat. I stared for a long time as he walked off into the distance. I tried to picture that somewhere inside him lurked the same passionate youth who once protested in the plaza all those years ago. But I couldn't see that young man now, not in Dept. Head Kim's hunched over shoulders at least. All I could see was the slowly fading silhouette of an elderly citizen.

And just like that, after ten months of being an intern, I became a regular employee at the academy.

13

AGE OF SELF-HELP

People who haven't been hired before won't know the joyous tradition of buying a friend a meal to celebrate. That was the motto for the day, even if it wasn't all that much to be excited about. And yet, Dabin seemed sincerely happy for me. In fact, seeing the way she got teary-eyed and would congratulate me every few seconds, I couldn't help but feel embarrassed for thinking we had been alienated from each other.

"I hope you go all the way to the top."

The inside of my nose began to tingle with a burning sensation when she said this.

I knew why Dabin had gone abroad to wander, why she eventually came back to Korea, why she accepted the first man who proposed to her and got married at such a young age. I also knew why—despite her unruly spirit—she was incapable of refusing her parents' pleas to have a wedding.

Dabin had been a twin. They were unusually identical, even as far as identical twins were concerned, and went everywhere together. It happened one summer's day in 1995 while she and her family were in Seoul to spend three days at a relative's house. The day before they left, the whole family visited a large department store. Having come from the provinces, they'd never seen anything like it. But that day, the department store collapsed. Dabin and her parents survived, but not her sister. The two of them were caught in a wall of gray debris, their small hands desperately sticking out of the rubble, like fern buds in the ground. But it was Dabin whom the first responder pulled out first. The moment Dabin's body broke free from the wall, the rest of it collapsed on her sister. Her hand was still outstretched toward Dabin when they recovered her body.

Dabin wanted to escape the memory of her sister but could never forget what happened that day at Sampoong Department Store. Such is the burden that all survivors of major disasters must bear. Whenever people looked at her, she could hear their eyes saying, "You owe it to her. You were pulled out first." Survivors with such a heavy burden cannot move forward. They wander through life with the knowledge of the sacrifice that made their existence possible, unable to live for themselves. That was the reason that Dabin went south of the equator to work under the hot Australian sun. That was why she eventually came back to her country to become a mother and give life to another human being.

As I thought about this, Dabin brought up Hyun-oh, my exboyfriend. It just so happened that Hyun-oh was also a friend of Dabin's husband. That's how she knew what he was up to. But of course, I already knew that he'd come back from England.

"Aren't you going to call him?"

Dabin was trying to bait me into talking about him, but I wasn't going to bite. I shook my head. In fact, I'd contacted him just after

Dabin first told me about his return. But I couldn't bring myself to tell her that.

* * *

A bag of Honeycomb Pizza Chips. All couples have at least one such object—an emblem of when they first fell in love. For us, it was a bag of Honeycomb Pizza Chips. On the way to school. At the subway station. A young man and woman sit next to each other, an appropriate amount of distance and two bags of chips separating them. His hand slips into her bag by accident. "Oh, sorry." "Not at all. Help yourself." "I see you like Honeycomb Pizza Chips." "What in the world gave you that idea?" "The train's here." "I can catch the next one. At least until you finish what you've started."

And thus, Honeycomb Pizza Chips had become special, a symbol of destined love.

Five years together, and hormones way past their expiration date. Fate as lopsided as an unbalanced seesaw. Job rejection after job rejection, she falls further and further behind, while he is hired on a fast track and sent abroad. Fights become more frequent. A job offer whose timing seems too perfect. Long distance. More fights. Makeups. More fights. Fall out. Breakup by email.

At the time, I'd thought our story was one of a kind, the kind of love you thought other people just couldn't understand. But with time, I realized it was nothing special. That didn't mean it hurt any less. My breakup with Hyun-oh seemed, to me, symbolic. Once he was gone, it felt like an entire part of my life had been severed from me. My years with him were the best of my life, the most splendid, the most beautiful. Tears formed in my eyes the moment I realized a period of my life had ended irrevocably. The love story had ended in failure, and all that was left was a melancholic where-are-they-now chapter.

Hyun-oh is sitting before me. For the most part, he looks the same. And yet, every time I catch a new habit or mannerism, I am painfully reminded that the years have turned us into strangers. The undercut he swore he'd never get. The type of long coat I wanted to buy for him, but which he said wasn't his style. Cologne, which he once claimed real men didn't wear. Then again, three years in a foreign country was more than enough time to develop new tastes, to change into a completely different person—I guess. He silently pushes the bowl of peanuts toward me. I look at his fingertips and am reminded of how round and soft they used to be. Habits and idiosyncrasies only I knew. Things that were once mine, but now only came back as fond memories.

But something even more fundamental had changed about him. And it wasn't the fact that he'd just handed me an invitation to his wedding, or that he'd done something contemptible that couldn't be washed away. If I had to put my finger on it, it was his answer when I asked him if he still ate those chips we used to love to share. He didn't. But then again, neither did I.

We said farewell. "Annyeong." My tone was upbeat as I spoke these two syllables, but inside, I was opening a locked door and pushing him out. I'd waited too long to write this epilogue. But feeling more relieved and emboldened than sad, I realized it was a perfect ending. Finally, it was over.

* * *

Not much changed after I became a regular employee. And Gyuok seemed indifferent to my promotion. He congratulated me sincerely, and I sensed no unease or begrudgery from him. He seemed to not care as long as he got paid above a certain amount. After I told Gyuok about what happened with Dept. Head Kim, he became lost in thought and didn't say anything.

"Gyuok, I'm sure you'll become a regular employee soon, too."

His response to this was quiet. "No, that wasn't my goal for coming here."

I could have asked him what he meant, but I didn't and lost my chance. And because of that, his comment remained like a faint echo in my mind.

Dept. Head Kim had left just before the end of the semester, leaving more work for us to do than ever. What didn't change, however, was that Gyuok and I were still expected to prepare lecture materials, move chairs, and stand in front of the copy machine for hours on end. Team Leader Yu was the most affected by Dept. Head Kim's sudden departure. She said she didn't want to hear anyone talk about her potential promotion to department head, but I could tell that she was excited about the opportunity to finally leave her mark on the company. I was exhausted because not only did I have to do the same work I did before but now I also had to sit down with Team Leader Yu to plan new courses. Among the many big moves she had planned for the academy, the biggest was a plot to use the money that would have gone to Dept. Head Kim's salary for hiring a new star lecturer.

Much like my little brother, Team Leader Yu was a pragmatist. As she designed the new courses for the upcoming summer semester, she emphasized that we needed to completely change the academy's obsession with the liberal arts.

"Lectures are no longer just places to learn theories and read books. People need to learn how to live."

"Learn how to live?"

Team Leader Yu nodded solemnly.

"I'm talking about self-help. It's the age of self-help, after all. That's what people want. People pay us a lot of money. It's only fair that we give them something in return, something that's worth the tuition. Self-help is way better than reading a bunch of useless liberal arts books that you're going to forget in a few months anyways. That's the trend these days. That's the direction we need to take the company."

And with that, it was decided; we were going to prepare an entire series of courses for self-improvement. I couldn't shake the feeling that our academy was beginning to look more and more like a commercialized culture center at a department store, but there was no stopping Team Leader Yu and her ambitions.

Dept. Head Kim's resignation left me in shock. He had just as good a reason to be angry at the world as I did. And I had a bad feeling that I was the reason he'd gotten fired. Gyuok seemed to be feeling just as guilty, although I couldn't be sure. I couldn't bring it up. It was too embarrassing to admit that not only had I been the person who gave Gyuok the idea but I was also the one who benefited from Dept. Head Kim's firing. On the upside, at least I would probably never have to look Dept. Head Kim in the eye again.

Most acquaintances disappeared like that, carried far away by the currents of time and fate. But every so often, you run into someone you never thought you'd meet again. And I was about to have just such an experience, only not with Dept. Head Kim. No, the person I was going to meet again was going to remind me of an older shame. Someone from a painful, faded memory, someone who taught me the true meaning of rage and despair.

* * *

Team Leader Yu busied herself recruiting famous figures in the field of self-help, dividing them into different specialties: housewives, office workers, retirees, etc. She tried to tackle all of it by herself, but when after a few days she ran into a brick wall, she had no choice but to ask me to recruit one of them myself.

"If we can land this woman, it'll only be a matter of time before people are flocking to the academy to take her class. We might get as many new students as when Professor Park first started teaching here."

"Who is she?"

"Kong Yun. Look her up if you don't know her. Either way, you'll need to do some research to make a pitch."

I'd heard of the name Kong Yun before. Intelligent and metropolitan, she was a popular guest on talk shows. That night, I picked up her book at the bookstore to read on my way home. It took me only an hour and a half to go from cover to cover, and when I put it down, I realized I'd wasted my 16,000 won. The story was one I'd heard a thousand times before. She'd had an impressive career at a big trading firm until one day when she started to doubt everything and quit. She then took the money she'd saved up for her future wedding as well as the security deposit from her apartment and spent it all traveling the world. A year later, after hopscotching around Europe, Africa, and South America, she arrived back at Incheon International Airport with nothing but a bag of clothes, 10,000 won, and a fresh start at life. I could say more, but I'm sure you get the picture.

The book was filled with the photos of her with friends she'd made around the globe. Photos of her learning tribal dances in Africa, of coffee-bean harvests in Brazil, of her own shadow under the Tuscan sun. Only in the last chapter did she finally give her advice to the young women of today. Write down your goals, visualize yourself achieving those goals, affirm yourself every morning—there was little you couldn't find in any other self-help book at your local bookstore. The last page of the book was dedicated to the affirmation she'd recited to herself every day "even and especially when things looked bleak," she emphasized.

> Everything will go the way I plan it to.
> The stars in the universe shine for me.
> I am special. I am unique. I am peerless.

Most of her advice seemed reasonable, but it was hardly something to write a whole book about. It was the kind of thing you'd read at a Starbucks while sipping on a Frappuccino on New Year's Day before "accidentally" leaving it on the windowsill for someone else to find. I studied the woman's portrait on the inside flap. A layered bob, an aquamarine two-piece dress that hugged her figure, and just enough makeup to bring out her best features. I could see why she'd become so famous. She knew how to make her life sound like a movie. She knew how to direct herself like a star.

The age group that Kong Yun most appealed to were women in their midthirties. Travel diaries masquerading as self-help books that told people to quit their jobs and chase their dreams just didn't work on anyone older who'd already settled into life's orbit. But the ability to appeal to this generation's youthful optimism and metropolitan vanity was part of why she was so successful.

As I mulled over her and her book, I had a sudden flash of inspiration and started writing the pitch for her class on the spot. While we would use her fame to appeal to students, I still needed a catchy course title and description. Something about looking back on one's life, and one last chance to escape . . . Eventually, this is what I came up with:

"Woman in the Mirror."

To start anew, one must reflect on the good and the bad. And to do that, one must start by looking in the mirror . . .

Words raced across the white expanse of my screen. In a matter of minutes, I finished writing the syllabus and sent it to Team Leader Yu.

"Not bad" was the first thing Team Leader Yu said to me when we saw each other the next day. And while it wasn't the praise I was hoping for, I knew coming from her, it was a good compliment. She then pointed at me like she had a gun in her hand and said, "Go get her!"

I edited the mock syllabus a bit more before attaching it to an empty email. Feeling that I would have a better chance recruiting her over email than by phone, I made the whole pitch electronically, in the most humble and polite tone I could manage. The entire email was no more than a dozen or so sentences, and yet, because of the knowledge that this was my first real project as a regular employee, it took me an hour to edit and revise it. But just as my eyelids started to droop from the exhausting task of rechecking my grammar, my finger suddenly pressed the "send" button, either on purpose or by mistake, I was too tired to tell which.

My heartbeat as I waited for her reply was unbearably fast.

I pressed the "check remittance" button impatiently, but it appeared that she had turned off that setting, preventing senders from knowing whether she'd read their email or not. I was anxious, but at the same time, I also had a good feeling about this—as though the reply she would eventually send me would be the start of my new career. Around dinnertime, her reply poked its head into my notifications. From the few words I could read in the notification, it appeared to be a polite reply. I immediately opened my mailbox and read her email. When I got to the following two lines, I read them over and over again, like a person might obsess over a text from a crush.

A lecture I can do.
Should we meet first to talk about it?

After a short back and forth, we decided to meet the following day at a book café near Hapjeong.

It was a weekday afternoon, and yet the café was humming with people as though it were a long weekend. The air was filled with jazzy tunes and the smell of coffee, and everyone was busy reading books or working on their laptops.

I found a seat in the corner of the café and sent a message to Kong Yun telling her that I'd arrived. I got a phone call as soon as I picked up a magazine to pass the time. No sooner did I speak into the receiver than I made eye contact with a woman sitting across the café from me. She looked just like the woman on the inside flap of the book I'd read the other night. I sent her a long-distance smile then walked over to her.

Kong Yun was sitting with her legs crossed on a couch, a tight purple dress squeezing her thighs together. As I got closer, my eyes were drawn to her gel nail polish, which was decorated with intricate patterns and glitter. We exchanged forced, awkward smiles—the kind people made when meeting someone for work.

"Nice to meet you. I'm Kong Yun."

She extended her hand toward me. It was uncommon for a woman to offer the first handshake, and even more so when the other person was also a woman. Her hand as I took it was so cold and clammy that it startled me. The way she gave my palm a good, long squeeze before relaxing her grip and retreating reminded me of the way a boa constrictor might slither away after strangling its prey.

"It's always strange when you finally meet someone you've only exchanged emails with. Nice to meet you. I'm Kim Jihye."

The way Kong Yun's eyes started to grow as she looked at me made me think I'd said something wrong. Not knowing how else to react, I just shrugged my shoulders as if to ask her what was wrong. Her eyes then squeezed into tight slits as though she'd just retrieved a fuzzy memory. Suddenly, an uncomfortable feeling spread throughout my body—an old but familiar feeling of unease and discomfort. Rising to the surface from the depths of my consciousness was a sharp and painful emotion, one that I'd thought I'd forgotten. She spoke at the exact moment I realized where this sensation was coming from.

"Do you remember me?"

Yes, that smile. How could I ever forget that smile. The day she first asked me my name, she made this same smile as she said, I'm Jihye. We have the same name. Let's be friends.

And now here she was, thirteen years later, standing in front me of and giving me that same smile.

"It's me. Jihye."

Her tone was full of conviction, as if there was only one person in the whole entire world with that name. Her voice resonated like tumbling ice, and her mouth was twisted into a smirk. My heart froze. It was her.

Jihye had never—not once—said the words "I'm Jihye, too." Nor was she "also Jihye." She always referred to herself as just "Jihye," no adverbs, no modifiers, nothing. While my name felt to me like a grain of sand on the beach, she treated her name like a proper noun that always had to be written in boldface, as though she were the true Jihye. The rest of us were just shadows and copies.

We were once classmates. On the attendance sheet, her name was written as Kim Jihye A, and mine, Kim Jihye B. But she never called me Jihye, not even Jihye B. My name from the moment I met her to the last time I saw her, was nothing more than the letter B.

thought we were friends."

She would always remind me of this just when I was about to forget it. It was as much of a conciliation as it was a form of psychological torture.

Jihye singled me out on the first day of high school. Because she'd just transferred schools, she had no friends and didn't know her way around the neighborhood. When she told me this, I couldn't help but offer to show her around. She immediately took me up on my offer and asked me to walk her home. But that wasn't all.

"I'm a bit shy, you see. Can't it be just the two of us?"

She meant for me to leave my friends to hang out with her. And the way she asked it made it hard to refuse. I told my friends that it would only be for a few days, but little did I know that those few days would irrevocably damage my relationship with them.

To this day, I don't know why she chose me. She didn't even know my name when she first approached me. Perhaps I was simply the first sucker she laid eyes on. Whatever the reason, from that day on, I ate lunch with her, walked home with her, and listened to her talk about her troubles.

In the beginning, she treated me like her best and only friend, always calling me "bestie" and texting me, "I love you" or "Goodnight." But I didn't remain her only friend for long. She was stunningly beautiful and had an aura that drew everyone's attention. So naturally, she was, with time, able to attract more friends to her—friends who were more in line with her standards. And when that happened, she didn't need to lean on me anymore.

She stopped asking me to walk her home and didn't tell me any more of her secrets. But there was one thing that didn't change: her constant requests. Whenever she asked me to do something for her, she would give me a smile and say, "I thought we were friends." Perhaps this was true at one point in time, but when eventually her requests turned into coldhearted demands, I knew we weren't friends anymore. I was her secretary, an errand girl, a handmaiden, just some loser kid who'd do anything to please her.

She'd ask me to do anything and everything for her. Most requests were nothing more than going to the convenience store to buy her snacks. Sometimes she made me sneak out during lunchtime just to pick up her preferred brand of sanitary pads—she was picky when it came to things like that. And other times, I had to deliver messages for her to other students. She even expected me to get her school supplies before she ran out.

And yet, Jihye never used me for money or physically abused me. She always paid me back for the things I bought, and sometimes she would even buy me small gifts to show her appreciation. On my birthday that year, she slipped an expensive stick of lip gloss and a handwritten card into my school bag. The dissonance confused me so much that I didn't know whether to love or hate her. The other kids would whisper among themselves and spread rumors about my relationship with Jihye, but I never got the chance to defend myself. I was, to her, an old but reliable tool, too useful to throw away but too rusty to show off. And whenever I showed reluctance, all she needed was to say the few words "I thought we were friends," and I would be right back in line. I couldn't find the courage to tell her that this wasn't how friends treated each other.

One day our homeroom teacher's cherished decorative elephant disappeared from the classroom. Our homeroom teacher, who was also the art teacher at school, loved decorating classrooms with all manner of art and figurines. He was such a hoarder, rumor had it, that his wife divorced him because of it. And yet, he seemed to lose no sleep over the rumors that students spread about his condition. Anyway, one day, he brought a glass elephant the size of a melon to class. I still remember the way he bragged about it, explaining that it was an expensive work of art he'd bought from a famous Taiwanese glassmaker, as though he were a preschooler during show-and-tell. He made the mistake, however, of leaving the elephant with his homeroom students instead of taking it back to his office with him. And thus, for the next several hours, as different teachers came to our classroom to teach us, the ridiculous-looking elephant had to endure our teasing and taunting. When we came back after gym time, however, the elephant was gone.

Because there were no CCTV cameras in the classroom, there was no way to catch the one responsible unless someone, either a witness or the culprit, confessed. Days turned into weeks, but our homeroom teacher showed no signs of giving up. Every day he would make us stay an extra thirty minutes after the last bell while all the other homerooms went home. Only medical and family emergencies were enough to get excused on time. With our eyes closed, we had to hear the teacher pace around the room as he lectured us. "It's not too late. Just raise your hand quietly, and we can all go home." And even as summer break drew near, he vowed to continue his hunt into the next semester, for as long as he had us under his thumb.

As this went on, I was still suffering from my role as Jihye's errand girl. I could feel myself slowly starting to disappear, and my relationship with her was becoming more and more subservient.

"Hey, B!"

I'd hear myself being summoned by Jihye like this several times in just one day. I had ceased to be known by the name Jihye. Even the other kids in our class called me B. Ironically, that was the first and last time in my life that I'd possessed a unique name. By then, Jihye had her own group of friends, and the kids I'd considered my friends before meeting Jihye, had now formed their own group without me. Even if I tried to join them, I had missed so much that I was basically a stranger. Aside from the rumors surrounding my relationship with Jihye, no one made fun of me or bullied me. But neither did anyone make a gesture of kindness. Before I knew it, I'd become the odd kid out at my own school. I ate alone, walked home alone, and did all the chores Jihye asked of me, alone. Then one day, I made up my mind to end it.

We were sitting across from each other at Baskin-Robbins. Between us were three different flavors of ice cream that Jihye had bought to share.

"Don't worry about paying me back," Jihye said as she lapped at the ice cream. "I don't thank you nearly enough. Anyway, what's it that you want to talk about?"

Looking down at the melting scoops of ice cream, I realized that she'd never asked me what my favorite flavor of ice cream was. Shoulders tense and words stuttering, I told her not to order me around anymore. Silence fell between us for a moment before Jihye slammed her spoon down on the table. She then rested her chin on her hand and stared at me for a long while.

"You know what? I thought we were friends. I thought we were *besties*."

"I used to think so, too. But I don't know anymore." I hated the way my voice sounded like I was apologizing.

The high-pitched laugh she made when I said this pinged around in my ears like a glass marble.

"Do you want to see my home?" she whispered to me as if telling a secret. "I haven't let anyone hang out with me at my home. How would you feel if you were the first?"

Jihye grabbed my hand before I could answer.

The place she took me was located behind the school, a dilapidated neighborhood scheduled for redevelopment. We walked and walked through the winding alleys until we stopped in front of a dark shack that looked abandoned.

Pushing through the creaking door and stepping into the house, Jihye said cheerfully, "This is my reality. Surprised?"

I said I wasn't, but because of the way my voice cracked, even to my ears, it sounded like I was surprised. I quickly followed her inside. The interior was a faded reddish brown and barely lit. The air was thick, and a pungent smell pierced my nostrils. Coming from inside the house was the sound of someone coughing—or rather hacking.

"That's Grandma. Wanna meet her?"

I shook my head, but Jihye had already grabbed my hand and was leading me further inside. When the door to the bedroom opened, I was met with a disturbing scene. An old woman with short gray hair was staring up at the ceiling, her mouth agape. The sound of her short, choppy coughing pierced the air as regularly as a metronome.

"I'm home, Grandma. This is my friend."

Jihye crouched on the garbage-littered floor and started stroking the dirty, wrinkled face of the woman. The old woman turned her head to look at me with moist eyes. I was so startled by what I was seeing—like I'd suddenly been thrust into a dark, alternate reality—that I couldn't help but cast my eyes downward.

"You don't have to stand on ceremony. She can't hear. Actually, I'm not sure what's wrong with her. But that's my guess after a couple weeks observing her."

The way Jihye talked about her supposed grandmother was as though she were introducing me to some diseased pet. There was an unsettling dissonance between the way she was affectionately stroking the old woman's greasy scalp and the coldhearted words coming out of her mouth.

"You mean, she's not your grandma?"

"Nope." Jihye seemed to be taunting me. "But I'm the one who found her. Not a single person has come to visit her since I arrived. She might as well be my grandma. Right?"

Immediately, I knew what she was insinuating. She was doing this abandoned old woman a favor by befriending her, just like she was doing me a favor by being my friend when no one else wanted me.

Jihye shot up from the ground and started fixing her hair in the cloudy mirror hanging on the wall.

"I did some snooping, and it seems like she's relatively well educated. She's got a high school diploma, not common for a woman her age, and was once a schoolteacher. She's even got two boys, believe it or not. I bet she never imagined that this was the fate awaiting her at the end of the line. But none of us can tell the future. In that sense, we're just like her."

The old woman stirred. It was at that moment that something familiar and shiny caught my eye. Noticing the change in expression on my face, Jihye leaned forward to pull the bedsheets over the object, but it was already too late.

"That's—" I stopped mid-sentence.

It was our homeroom teacher's glass elephant. The elephant, which was being held tight to the old woman's chest as though it were some holy object, was bobbing up and down to the rhythm of her wheezing.

Jihye let out a quiet sigh. "She needs it more than that stupid prick. Besides, elephants bring good fortune and long life."

"But that doesn't belong to her."

"You're right. Well, you *were* right. It didn't belong to her. But it does now."

Not knowing what to say, I dropped my gaze again. When I did this, I became aware that my chest was rising and falling rapidly. Even if Jihye couldn't see this, it would be hard to miss the loud sound of my breathing filling the room.

"Are you disappointed in me?" Jihye's pupils flickered. Her voice was kind, but I could tell that she was angry.

"No!" These words flew out of my mouth.

"I know I did the wrong thing. But I just never had the chance to put it back where it belonged."

I thought about the punishment our class had endured for the last few months, the countless hours spent sitting in silence, listening to our teacher's angry lectures. I also remembered how Jihye had complained to me about how everyone was suffering because of one selfish person. My face was becoming red, and I was incapable of saying anything.

Jihye opened her eyes wide and approached me, bringing her face within inches of mine.

"No, you *are* disappointed. Just look at how you're blushing."

"No . . ."

"No, no. You *are*. I can tell. All I wanted was to do something nice for an old lady, and you're not even trying to hear me out. I always gave you special consideration. But here you are, trying to end our friendship one-sidedly. I bet you never considered me your friend."

Jihye turned away from me and went over to the old woman to stroke her hair.

"I'm hurt," she said in a low voice.

I couldn't take this. All I wanted was to leave this place as soon as possible. But before I knew it, I was pleading with her.

"What do I need to do to make you believe me?" I asked.

Jihye's hand paused. She turned to me with a pleased look. Her eyes were saying, "So, you finally understand?"

"Prove your loyalty to me. Put this back in the classroom. Do it for me. That much you can do for a friend, can't you?"

I looked down at the elephant as the old woman held it tightly in her arms. It'd been watching us this whole time, and yet never said a word.

Just like Jihye, I chose gym time to return the elephant. Today, we were playing badminton in groups of two on the sports field. The early summer heat and pollen in the air was turning my skin hot and itchy.

I sneaked out of the line and headed back to the classroom. I gripped the elephant that was inside my bag. It was so big that it was hard to grab with just one hand. My heart was racing, and my face was on fire. I placed the elephant on the corner of the teacher's desk. Now all I had to do was return to gym. But when I turned around, I met eyes with someone—a student who had skipped gym to take a nap. When we made eye contact, I stepped back in shock and bumped the teacher's desk. The elephant teetered left and right like a roly-poly toy before finally crashing to the floor. The elephant's body broke into a million sharp fragments that skidded across the floor in every direction. Students from other classrooms came to see what the sound was. One after another, they filed into the classroom. They looked on in shock as I stood there like a statue, only with trembling hands.

That day just before the final bell rang, the homeroom teacher ordered me to stand up in front of the whole class. He berated me, asking why I stole his elephant, but I just clenched my jaw and didn't say anything. He then hit me over the head several times with his attendance board. The shock caused tears to form in my eyes. Several students were cursing at me under their breath. I looked toward Jihye and pleaded with my eyes for help. But she was reading a book, a headset covering her ears. Her head was bobbing back and forth gently, as though she hadn't a care in the world, as if she'd had nothing to do with me nor the elephant.

I never had another chance to confront Jihye about what happened. The incident occurred too close to summer vacation, and by the start of the next semester, she'd already transferred schools again, following her father who was in the military. And thus, the aftermath of the glass elephant incident was mine to deal with. For the rest of my time in high school, I was known as a "lying, stealing bitch." That's what the other kids would shout at me when I walked through the halls. Thankfully, their bullying didn't last long. One day, when someone threw a rock at me and called me a name, I screamed and started pulling at my hair. After that, no one wanted to mess with the "crazy girl." The trauma of it all caused me to withdraw deep into myself. My current habit of always walking with my head down and never looking people in the eye were psychological scars left from those painful years.

I went to that poor neighborhood just once after Jihye left. But the entire area had turned into a construction site, atop which they were hurrying to erect a tall apartment building. No matter how hard I looked, I couldn't find any trace of that old woman. It was as if she and that dark shack were nothing but mirages that only existed in my mind.

The memories of it followed me even into adulthood. I would sometimes have nightmares about picking up the pieces of the glass elephant off the floor, screaming, "It wasn't me! It wasn't me!" The day I reunited with Jihye, or Kong Yun, I had that same dream. But no matter how loud I screamed, no one was listening. The other students just stood in front of me as though they couldn't hear me. I screamed until I collapsed on the ground in tears. Then suddenly, I felt the warmth of someone's hand on my head. When I looked up, I discovered Jihye standing in front of me. She was wearing a long white nightgown that fluttered in the wind. "It's okay. Even if no one knows, I do. I know it wasn't you." I moved into her arms and cried into her chest. But then a bony sensation caused me to lift my head. A hideous face was looking back at me. It was the face of the old woman, dark and wrinkled. That was the last thing I remembered before being jolted awake.

RUN

I stood under the shower as a stream of hot water fell onto the crown of my head. But by the time the water trickled down to my toes, it was already cold. My body had yet to stop shaking.

She'd changed her legal name from Kim Jihye to Kim Kong Yun. In fact, she disliked her old name so much that she'd paid money to a professional to choose a new name for her. The name Kong Yun, it turned out, was what she used for work and writing.

"Jihye was too commonplace," she said with a cold laugh.

She and I didn't say much to each other after that. I pinned my trembling hand beneath my thigh as I explained the syllabus to her and the details of her payment.

"You know, I still think of you sometimes," she said before leaving. "I've always wondered if you resented me for what happened. But we were so young."

She gave me a slight smirk, her mouth turning sideways as a deep dimple formed on her cheek. I'd always crumbled when confronted with that smile. It had been thirteen years, and still, all I could do was just smile back at her like a shy child. When she was gone, the realization that nothing had changed, that I was still a loser, zapped all the energy from my body.

I curled up in the shower and let the water pelt me like a storm. Thirteen years later, and yet it felt like I hadn't grown up at all.

Secretly, I wished her class would be canceled due to a lack of interest. So it was a slap in the face when I learned that her class had sold out in record time. After showing her to her classroom with an amiable expression on my face, I came back in the middle of her lecture to sneak a peek through the window. To my surprise, she was unlike other lecturers and didn't waste time by making students give self-introductions on the first day of class. She looked completely at home in front of the large audience, waving her hands with large gestures and projecting her voice to the back of the class. Her face had changed a lot. She'd always been beautiful, but her new nose and double eyelids made her almost unrecognizable. If she hadn't said something, I would not have realized it was her. If only.

"What's wrong?" Gyuok, who'd sneaked up on me, tapped me on the shoulder.

I just gave him a powerless smile. If there was nothing I could do, it was better not to mention anything.

Whenever I was feeling down, I would join the boys for drinks to cheer myself up. Even though we hadn't performed a prank for some time now, it was still refreshing to hang out and talk. But the good feelings only lasted for as long as I was with them. That day after saying goodbye, I left the bar and was immediately reminded that I was still a failure. The fact that I still walked back home from work every day with tired footsteps meant that I'd failed to change anything. I liked thinking that we could change the world. But who was I kidding? I couldn't even change myself. It was all just for show.

I dreaded running into Kong Yun at the academy so much so that I reorganized my entire week around her Wednesday lectures. Wednesday felt like Friday nights, and Saturday morning through the following Wednesday was a slow progression of ever-worsening symptoms that started with a sore throat and progressed through coughing, a fever, and even rashes. Just hearing her footsteps coming down the hallway was enough to make my body start presenting the symptoms of a mysterious illness.

Gyuok, on the other hand, became quite chummy with Kong Yun, and eventually they would even joke with each other. But it seemed like Kong Yun was the more interested of the two. Whenever she saw Gyuok, she would go to him to strike up a conversation, and sometimes she would even buy him food or a drink. Every time I heard the two of them laughing down the hallway, I felt my head retracting into my shoulders. I became cold toward Gyuok, even though I knew he didn't know any better, and day by day the fire inside me that wanted me to quit grew larger and larger. But then one Friday night, someone decided to pour oil on that fire.

* * *

I thought it was supposed to be a company dinner. You know, the kind that only company employees were invited to. But when I arrived late to the restaurant, I discovered that several lecturers were in attendance. Even Gyuok, who didn't usually come to company dinners, was present. A little after I arrived, Kong Yun showed up as well. I quickly got myself a glass of beer and started drinking so I could avoid having to watch her and Gyuok get comfortable with each other. But perhaps this was a mistake, because once I was a bit tipsy, I lost sight of my goal and looked up, accidentally making eye contact with her. She maintained eye contact with me as she made an exaggerated facial expression, lifting her glass toward me for a two-person toast. I lifted my glass without saying anything as she crashed her glass against mine. Immediately after this, she turned to everyone and called for their attention.

"Did you know? Jihye and I used to go to high school together."

"Really?" Team Leader Yu asked.

Kong Yun then looked at me in feigned surprise. "You didn't tell them?"

"Oh, well . . . It wasn't really relevant to work." I could feel myself mumbling.

"Yeah? We were really close. We ate lunch together and walked home together. I owe so much to her."

"What exactly do you owe to her?" It was Gyuok.

"I don't know. It's like an indentured friendship."

The way Kong Yun said this made it clear to everyone that there was some long juicy backstory to be told. Sure enough, everyone started asking what kind of debt she was talking about.

"Do you want to tell them, Jihye?" Kong Yun asked this as if to test me.

Instead of answering, I picked up my cell phone and held it up to my ear. "Hello? Yes, yes." I turned my body away from the group, muttered a couple of nonsense sentences into the receiver, and then pretended to hang up the phone.

"I've gotta get going. My friend's waiting for me."

"Who is it? A boyfriend, perhaps?" Her shrill voice pierced through the noise of the bar and reached everyone's ears.

"It must be," Team Leader said. "We've never seen him, though. He is your boyfriend, right, Jihye?"

"Yes, he's my boyfriend." I was already walking toward the exit as I grumbled this.

Loneliness followed me all the way to the bar. This was my first time drinking together with Mr. Jeong-jin. We'd only ever met for lunch and coffee; I'd never used him as an excuse to get drunk. In fact, this was my first time drinking alone at a bar. It was the same LP bar where we all gathered that first night. There weren't many patrons, and I sat with my back against the wall as I lifted the beer bottle to my lips. I must have been thoroughly intoxicated, because the sensation of the bitter liquid making its way down my throat felt detached, as though it was happening inside someone else's body. *I'm going to quit.* That's what I decided. Tomorrow, I was going to tell Team Leader Yu that I quit. I took another swig of beer as I tried to calm my mind. Quitting was my only option for getting out of this shitty predicament.

"You never listen. I thought I told you to stop meeting that Jeong-jin guy."

Gyuok had sneaked up on me again. He'd already taken a seat beside me.

"What are you doing here again?" I asked with slurred speech.

"Well, I was going to confess my feelings for you. But then I heard you were meeting your boyfriend. So, I came to check out the competition." Gyuok chuckled.

"I'm not in the mood for jokes." I paused before continuing. "I'm going to quit."

"Quit? Why?"

"The situation is such that I have to quit."

"I see . . ."

Gyuok exhaled and then started tapping his fingers on the table as if he found this amusing.

"You've finally got your chance, and you're just going to quit? I guess you've got an easy life."

"I've never had an easy life." I sneered at Gyuok. "In fact, it's the exact reason that I'm quitting. I'm tired. I don't want to have to think about dreams or aspirations anymore. I'm sick and tired of being crushed by people who have it easier than me. Do you know what I hate? I hate when people tell me to try harder, to compete. I'm tired of trying harder and competing. That's all I've done my whole life. And yet here I am. For thirty years I've been trying harder and competing, and this is all I've got to show for it."

I was yelling at Gyuok, as though he were the root of all my problems. I fanned myself with my hands as I caught my breath. Gyuok put a handful of corn snacks into his mouth and started munching on them. He only responded to me after he was done chewing.

"I've wanted to ask you something for some time now. Is it okay if I take this opportunity to ask?"

"Do what you want. You're already asking questions."

"You seem to think that you're moving toward something. Do you really think that's what you're doing? Or are you just pretending to not know that you're actually running from something?"

I racked my brain for a moment to unravel the tangled ball of words he'd just tossed in my lap. I hated Gyuok and his abstruse way of speaking. Why couldn't he just get to the point? Gyuok continued before I could answer him.

"If you've never thought about it, take tonight to sleep on it." He then leaned across the table and whispered into my ear. "And stop seeing Mr. Jeong-jin. It's not a healthy relationship."

I staggered my way home. I stumbled through the door and barely got my shoes off before running to the bathroom. I heaved several times, but nothing came up. All I wanted to do was vomit, but I couldn't even manage that. What did the world have against me? Why couldn't it just let me have my way, just this once? Feeling sorry for myself, I slumped down on the floor and let out a tearless wail. Perhaps I was too drunk to cry. I used both hands to pull myself up to the sink and look into the mirror. Staring back at me was a thirty-year-old straggler. But I wasn't really a straggler. You can't fall behind if you've never been ahead, just like you can't be in a slump if you've never experienced the high of summiting a mountain. No, I was just someone who'd been living day to day, doing just enough to get by. I did as much as my personality allowed me to. That was who I was.

This was the conclusion I came to while looking into the mirror. Nothing had ever gone the way I planned. I always put things off when it came time to make a change. I would never break up with Mr. Jeong-jin, and I would never turn in my letter of resignation like I wanted to. Perhaps that was what Gyuok meant when he accused me of running.

16

CONFIRMATION
OF EXISTENCE

Kong Yun was far from dependable. By the midway point of the semester, she'd already canceled two of the contracted twelve classes, and each time this happened, we had to issue the students refunds, as was company policy. After the first canceled class, I cautiously reminded her that it would be deducted from her next paycheck, but the way Kong Yun said she understood, without hesitation, was as though it didn't bother her in the slightest. Her demeanor let everyone know that she didn't need our money. And yet, because she gave it her all when she did make it to class, we had yet to hear any complaints from students. Some might call it talent, but from management's point of view, it was a giant red flag. She was barely on time, and never picked up her phone. Worst of all—at least in my opinion—was the special request she made to the academy. Every day before class, she required us to prepare her a cup of coffee; her reason was that she was just too busy to stop at a local coffee shop on her way to the academy.

It would be an understatement to say Kong Yun loved her coffee. And she was picky, too, always claiming that we couldn't expect her to give a proper lecture if it wasn't prepared the way she liked it. The coffee shop of her preference was a seven-minute walk from the academy. Most coffee chains had a branch at every street corner, but this chain didn't have very many locations because it had just recently broken into the Korean market from abroad. And fourteen minutes of walking, plus however long it took to order the coffee, was more than enough to get angry about.

Anyway, her order was a hot americano with three shots of espresso. And most important, it had to be served in her special tumbler.

If Kong Yun had asked me specifically to get her the coffee, I would have found some way to refuse. The problem was that the request came through Team Leader Yu.

"So in the future, always have Ms. Kong Yun's coffee ready for her when she arrives," Team Leader Yu said as she thrust Kong Yun's silver tumbler into my hands.

"You know, we don't need to do this for her. And besides, I'm not an errand girl."

Team Leader Yu had no way of knowing the true reason for my refusal to do this, and thus interpreted it as a prideful rejection of her authority.

"Well, well. Look who's all grown up. I guess you think you're special now that you're a regular employee. But no one can get through life only doing what they agree with, Jihye. Kids these days act like they don't know that. We do these things, Jihye, because if we don't the world will stop spinning. Here, give it to me. I can do it if you don't want to."

I didn't want to make this misunderstanding any bigger than it needed to be, nor did I want to fight with her. I changed my answer and said I'd do it.

One day, Kong Yun's students started coming out of the classroom about halfway through her two-hour lecture. Judging from the bags on their shoulders, it didn't look like they were just taking a break. There were no half days scheduled on the syllabus, and she hadn't mentioned anything about it to us beforehand. Even the students seemed confused by her ending class early. I went inside the classroom to find Kong Yun packing her bags. When I asked her what was going on, she gave me a smile as she explained that she had to go to a signing event for her new book. She said she simply "forgot" to mention it to us.

"This puts the academy in a really difficult position," I said. "'I forgot' just isn't good enough. This is the third time that something like this has happened. Your actions reflect really poorly on the academy."

I knew I had every right to call Kong Yun out on this. I was an adult, and this was my job. But I never expected what she'd say next.

"That's why I want you to lie for me. Just tell the front office I had a family emergency. Don't be like this. We're friends."

"I can't make excuses for you. If it's really a book-signing event, there will be pictures and videos of it online. Why lie when they're going to find out anyway? Instead of lying and making excuses, why don't you think about how you're going to apologize to the academy and your students? If you really just 'forgot' about it, the right thing to do is to tell the front office the truth."

I could feel my voice trembling as I spoke.

"Yeah? Well, I don't have the time for that right now. But Jihye, why are you so strict?"

"This is work."

The way Kong Yun raised her eyebrows was as if a switch had been flipped in her brain, from defense to offense.

"Right, work. Let me tell you something about *work*. My coffee? You got it wrong today. I specifically told you people that I don't drink coffee unless it's in my tumbler. Not only did you get it in a to-go cup, but you also threw it on my desk. You saw it spill everywhere, but you left without even saying sorry. And this isn't the first time something like this has happened. Last time, the coffee you got me was so cold, I thought it was an iced americano. You think this is just another coffee run, don't you? *That's* why you're irritable. What you don't understand is that coffee is an integral part of my lecture prep. I thought I made this clear. I don't know how anyone likes teaching at this academy. You people are so disrespectful to teachers. Anyway, be more careful in the future. You can tell the front office whatever you want. Either way, you have no power, and I only listen to people who do."

And with that, she left.

My mind went blank as though someone had highlighted all the files in my brain and pressed delete. Feeling my legs go weak, I fell backward into one of the classroom chairs. I looked around at the chairs strewn about the classroom. The antique chair that Kong Yun sat in at the front of the classroom was half pushed in and askew toward the entrance.

I recalled the time Gyuok philosophized about chairs. He assumed I existed down here in these chairs and claimed that I could go up there if I only had the courage to do so. But in reality, none of these chairs were for me. My job was to come in when class was over and clean up everyone else's mess.

"Something on your mind?" Gyuok had come into the room to see what was wrong.

"I'm thinking about how long I have to keep living like this."

Gyuok pursed his lips and quietly looked around the room. He seemed to be trying to figure out what it was I was talking about. "What do you mean?"

"I mean bottling up everything I want to say and then shooting myself in the foot. I can't remember ever not being like this. I'm such a joke, talking about changing the world, when I can't even change myself. I'm shaking my finger at the sky when the real problem is down here, staring me right in the face."

"Why don't you just try to do what you want to do? Don't think about whether you can or can't do it." Gyuok paused before continuing. "I know you can do whatever you set your mind to, Ms. Jihye."

I couldn't keep living like this. Actually, I could. Sure, I might get frustrated from time to time and threaten to quit, but eventually I'd just return to the same routine. And yet, I wanted to stop the cycle. I was tired of standing around and not saying anything while I cleaned up other people's messes and took the blame for them.

"I have somewhere I need to be."

These words left my lips before I could even finish my train of thought. Gyuok tried to stop me, but I was already headed out the door.

Engraved outside a large bookstore were a few inspiring words. "People make books. Books make people." Once upon a time, merely being in the proximity of a bookstore excited me. Back then, I thought books would make me a better person. But now, I couldn't even remember the last time I'd stepped in a bookstore to buy something I wanted to read.

The place was so packed with shoppers that I had to push people aside just to make a walking lane for myself. As I wandered the store, I eventually saw an even denser crowd of people gathered in the distance. Kong Yun sitting in the middle of the crowd. There she was, a fresh layer of makeup on, smiling and shaking hands with fans as she signed copies of her new book. There she was, that woman who'd made a career out of living a life that others envied. But to me, she was just a shadow cast across my life. I had to get out from under that shadow. I pushed my way to the front of the line. She looked up when she noticed I didn't have her book in my hand.

"Apologize," I said as we made eye contact. I could feel my voice reverberating from deep inside my chest.

A momentary look of surprise appeared on her face before turning into a sneer. "What?"

"For everything. For canceling class. For making me buy coffee for you. And for what you . . . For what you did to me back then . . ."

Kong Yun raised her eyebrows as if she didn't know what I was talking about. But soon, I heard an "Ah—" followed by a sharp cackle. She rested her chin on her hand and looked up at me with a gentle smile.

"So that's why you chased me here," she said. "And don't criticize *me* for skipping work. Just think of all the work you could be doing right now instead of coming here to embarrass me. You know, I think you should take my class. Do you know why your life turned out this way, Jihye? It's because you chose to live like this."

Something was stuck in my throat. My mouth was quivering. Kong Yun let out a sigh. There was a look of cheap pity in her eyes.

"Have you ever dreamed of being anything better than what you are right now, Jihye? Once you've asked yourself that and taken a good look in the mirror, then maybe you can ask me for an apology."

I could hear a murmur from the crowd. People took pictures and videos of us. Store security hurried toward me. Wearing a derisive sneer, Kong Yun ran her hand through her hair. The man behind me who was waiting to get his copy signed cleared his throat before nudging me out of the way. The way she immediately turned her attention to him with a smile was as though I was just another fan.

I left the crowd in a hurry, practically running. I could see people staring at me as I left. Or perhaps they weren't looking at me—after all, someone like me was just an object in the background to them. These people didn't care about me. This realization made the embarrassment of what had just happened all the more painful. I couldn't see where I was going because of the tears blurring my vision. Suddenly, someone's body hit mine like a wall. When I looked up, Gyuok's fuzzy face was staring down at me. As soon as I realized it was him, the tears turned into sobs. I was trying to not make a scene, but the sound of my sobbing was seeping out of my body like the sound of gurgling water. He didn't ask any questions and simply held me by the shoulders, as though he'd seen everything. He led me somewhere, but I couldn't tell where. I just covered my mottled face and let his hands guide me through the crowd.

A door opened and closed. The hum of people all but disappeared. Now the only thing filling the space was my own howling. Gyuok pressed down on my shoulders, seating me. We were in the fire emergency stairwell.

"I came because I was afraid you were about to do something." Gyuok spoke as though he were making excuses for himself. "I got worried when you didn't respond to my calls."

"I couldn't do it." I was shaking. "I had something I needed to say. I was going to let it all out. But it didn't go the way I thought it would. I looked even more pathetic than if I hadn't said anything. All I did was confirm how worthless of a person I am."

I could barely speak, and my tears were coming out as snot now. I had to pause every few seconds to sniffle.

"You will be if you keep talking about yourself like that."

Gyuok offered me a handkerchief as he said this. I slowly lifted my chin to look at him. His facial expression was gentle and kind, not at all like the insult he'd just thrown my way.

"But you should find comfort in the fact—" Gyuok paused and lowered his voice. "That we're all worthless. In the end. People are such pitiful creatures. Even the ones who like to pretend they're special and have it easy are having a hard time when you put them under a microscope. We're all struggling just to get confirmation that we exist, whatever way we can."

"How do you do that?" I asked, still choked up. "I don't even know who I am. What existence is there to confirm?"

Suddenly, a soft and warm energy encompassed me. "That question—" Gyuok was hugging me. How could someone so large and rough feel so warm and gentle? He lowered his voice further. "That question is one you're going to be asking yourself for the rest of your life. It's not just going to answer itself with old age. Loneliness, self-doubt, the purpose of life. Whenever you think about these things, you'll feel tormented and terrified that there are no answers, that you'll never figure it out. But there's something even scarier than not knowing. And that's going through life without ever asking. Most people avoid these questions because not only is asking them painful but it also seldom leads to definitive answers. Once you start asking, you'll always be doubting yourself and searching for answers that don't exist—"

"Stop, stop. Just stop!" I couldn't take it anymore and screamed at him. "I don't need words right now. I don't need explanations or logic. I don't need life lessons."

When I was done, I rubbed my face in his chest, soaking his flannel shirt with my tears. "Sorry, sorry." Gyuok's voice was heavy as he apologized to me. His plush chest made it feel like I'd entrusted my body to a giant marshmallow. I wanted to fall asleep like this. Now that I'd stopped crying, I could hear the footsteps and voices of people shopping for books beyond the iron door. And yet I felt like I was in a completely different space from that world, as though I was drifting in the warm ether. This peaceful, pleasant feeling washed over my body, slowly pushing away the sadness and embarrassment.

When my breathing steadied and I pulled my body away from his, I could see that he needed a new shirt. It hadn't been awkward when we were holding each other, but now that we were apart again, I felt strange. We looked each other in the eye.

"That was nice," I said, letting my careless emotions get the better of me.

"I'm glad." Gyuok said this with a smile, as though he'd had no part in the matter. "Should we go out for a beer? With all the tears you've shed, we need to get some fluids in you."

"But beer's a diuretic," I said, even though I knew this wasn't the time to nitpick his medical knowledge.

"So you don't want to go?"

"I'll go as long as you don't invite anyone else. Like last time."

Again, I'd let my careless emotions get the better of me, but this time, it was even worse.

Gyuok's eyes momentarily became wide with shock before he nodded slowly.

* * *

Chet Baker was singing a solo version of "Blue Room." Baker had a talent for making even the most cheerful tunes sound lonely and somewhat uneasy. It didn't matter if he was singing or playing the trumpet; he could do it with either. Just listening to his velvety sound, you'd think he was an academic obsessed with jazz. But as it turned out, he was a serious drug addict. While some musicians did drugs to make music, Baker made music to do drugs. That's how much of a junkie he was. All these useless factoids—things I'd learned while standing at the scanner copying lecture materials— were spilling out of my head. But right now, that wasn't important. In this confined space, Baker—who died the same year I was born, it just so happened—was performing a concert for two. Cheap, convenience store wine was trickling down the back of my throat, sending sweet sensations to the rest of my body.

Gyuok's apartment was a nerd's cave. The shelves were stacked with vintage LPs, heavily foxed books, and old Gundam figurines. Wine-bottle corks and soju-bottle caps littered every surface in the apartment. And yet, despite the hodgepodge of junk, the place had a certain harmony to it. I don't know what I'd imagined his apartment to look like, but this interior fit his personality perfectly. What I liked most, however, was the fact that it was just him and me.

Baker's song ended, and on came Bill Evans performing "My

Foolish Heart" on the piano. Evans's gentle and well-mannered fingers were, as they were known to do, plucking beautiful, transparent melodies from the piano. Sound waves rose inside my chest one after another. I quietly studied Gyuok—lips, fingers, those thick eyelashes. When we made eye contact, he smiled at me with his gentle gaze. It made my heart ache. And then a shadow suddenly cast itself across his face.

"I'm a mess," he began. "I might talk like I've got it all figured out, but I can never express my true self. Some people get caught up in the past. But I'm failing to see the present because I'm caught up in the future. And worst of all, I'm always trying to justify myself. I've convinced myself that I'm making the right choice. But that's only because it's the only way I can rest easy at night and not suffer from nightmares of regret and guilt."

These incoherent musings of a drunk man sounded like background noise to the drowsy music. Gyuok stopped talking to whistle a harmony to the main line. The sweet air from his lips merged with the song and tickled my ears. I lost myself staring at his lips. I wanted to interlock mine with his. My face became hot to the touch. I knew I was seconds away from doing something stupid. To stop myself, I poured some more wine into my mouth and swallowed. I bit my lip several times, holding back the words forming in my mouth, before at last I couldn't hold them back anymore.

"Gyuok—"

He turned to look at me.

"I think I like you."

This was the first time I'd ever confessed my feelings to someone like this. What had come over me? As I thought this to myself, I dropped my head and stared at the floor for a while. I couldn't hear

Gyuok's whistling anymore. I worked up the courage to look up at him. He didn't look surprised. No, his facial expression was somewhat sad, as though he felt sorry for me. He was just quietly gazing at me the way a compassionate person might pity a wounded animal.

"Me? But why? I don't have anything."

"Does that mean I can't like you? I know everyone else cares about money and nice things, but there's no reason for us to have to think like that."

I knew I was being presumptuous using the word "us" like this. Neither did I like my argumentative tone. But I couldn't help but raise my voice; I was angry because his defensive posturing felt like a rejection.

Instead of arguing with me, Gyuok chose another path. "What if there were something that I was hiding from you, Ms. Jihye? Something I couldn't tell you, at least not right now. Would you still feel the same?"

"I don't know. All I know is—"

I didn't bother finishing my sentence. What happened next was all my own doing. As I leaned forward, my hair draped across his shoulders and covered both our faces. His faint breathing tickled my lips. The kiss tasted of mint and wine. It was a long, sweet, silent kiss, the kind that would be perfect as the last scene of a movie before credits rolled. As we kissed, my consciousness started to fade. But just before I blacked out, I had the odd feeling that this would be our last kiss. And yet, that didn't make me want to let go. If anything, it made me want to hold on for just a little bit longer.

17

ROMANCE NO MORE

When I opened my eyes, Gyuok was gone. On the table was some milk and a piece of toast that was still warm. Remembering the kiss from last night, the hairs on the back of my neck stood up. I could still feel the sensation of his fingers running along the back of my neck up through my hair. There was no more romance that night. The words Gyuok said about having nothing bounced around inside my head as we kissed. And when I finally took my lips from his, he didn't hold on to me. I tried to get up to leave, only to stagger and fall back into my chair. That was all I could remember.

Lying next to the plate of toast was a folded piece of paper. I couldn't help but feel disappointed when I opened it. The only thing inside was a large smiley face and nothing else. Without even touching the toast, I left the apartment in a hurry. While that drawing could have been interpreted many ways, to me at least, it could mean only one thing. "Last night was a mistake," he seemed to be telling me. "Let's act like it never happened."

After that night, we remained friends. The chemistry between us—if any had ever existed to begin with—had all but disappeared, and all that was left was an awkward and uncomfortable friendship. At first, I tried to make eye contact with him, but eventually, I averted my eyes whenever we crossed paths.

I was the one who had made a move on him. The only reason we had kissed was because he hadn't rejected me. And when I pulled away, he didn't pull me back. Perhaps he was just being considerate. Perhaps he was just trying to be there for me, like a good friend would be. In the end, we had nothing, just as he'd said. I almost felt relieved when I thought about it like this. Perhaps we'd saved ourselves from getting sucked into a risky experiment. But even so, I felt dejected and embarrassed. Now, there was only one thing left to do. I had to stand my ground. I had to own my mistake. I wasn't going to run away.

We still met at the copy machine, moved chairs together, and saw each other in ukulele class. Now that it was fall semester, he and I were taking Intermediate Ukulele from the same instructor as before. Currently, we were learning to play the song "All of Me." Originally written by Frank Sinatra, the song was about telling someone to take everything from you if they loved you. Taken literally, the lyrics were somewhat terrifying.

> *Take my lips, I wanna lose them*
> *Take my arms, I'll never use them*

While people always sang about idiots in love, in reality, everyone was doing calculus before allowing themselves to fall in love. After all, stupid love today was painful love tomorrow—regretful and embarrassing.

While the conclusion to our romance was depressingly anticlimactic, the same couldn't be said for my feud with Kong Yun. She hadn't changed, but I had. Sure, I ran away and cried in a stairwell that day at the bookstore, but after that, I stopped avoiding her. Even the symptoms of cold sweats and tremors that used to happen whenever I sensed her presence disappeared completely.

Now there was just one thing left to do. I waited for my chance to address everyone, and a few days later when she came into the office carrying lecture materials, I got the opportunity to do just that.

"Everyone, I have something to say," I said in a loud voice.

They all looked at me. Even Kong Yun. No, even *Jihye*.

"I am not friends with Ms. Kong Yun, whose real name is Kim Jihye. And I've never been friends with her. I had hoped I'd never run into her again, but I guess life doesn't always go as planned. I just wanted to set the record straight so that no one mistakes us for friends. We are colleagues. Nothing more, nothing less. That is all."

Everyone's jaws dropped. Kong Yun let out a scoffing sound, but her face had already turned bright red. I didn't say any more and walked out of the office. As I made my way to the door, I thought I saw Gyuok crack a smile.

Two days later, Kong Yun informed the office that she would be quitting before the end of the semester. Among other things, she made the excuse that she had to promote her new book. They tried to stop her, but she held fast and offered to refund the academy the signing bonus she'd received. The last time Kong Yun visited the academy, Team Leader Yu got up in her face, waving her finger at her. "This is completely unprofessional!" And now that she was on the blacklist of Team Leader Yu, who had a lot of connections in the field, Kong Yun would have to hear that she was an unreliable lecturer for the foreseeable future. I hadn't spoken up with the intent to damage her career, but it is what it is.

Anyway, that incident taught me an important lesson. You can change things by simply speaking your mind rather than remaining quiet. In that sense, I was grateful to Gyuok, even though we had exchanged that embarrassing kiss.

It became harder and harder to see Gyuok. He would head home straight after work and became noticeably more reticent. Sometimes, he would even skip ukulele class. Naturally, our secret meetings also became less frequent. But it wasn't just Gyuok. Mr. Nam was busy nursing his daughter, who'd been admitted to the hospital with a severe cold, and Muin was preparing for a writing competition. I was starting to get the sense that I would soon leave this place. It was a phone call one Sunday morning that made that premonition into a reality.

* * *

When the phone first rang, I ignored it, thinking it was just my alarm clock, and continued to lay curled up under the covers for more than twenty minutes. A while later, I got a text message. It was from a number I didn't recognize, and they said they would be sending me an email with more information. Hoping it wasn't spam, I opened my inbox. The letter was from a company that I'd recently applied to for a job. Apparently, I'd made it to the final interview.

The sun was beating down on the quiet residential neighborhood. I saw several low-rise apartment buildings made of red brick, and lining the streets were small restaurants that had been converted from residential buildings. I walked for a while until I came upon a quaint building painted orange. I climbed the stairs outside the building until I reached a door on the third story, posted outside of which was a wooden sign with the words EMPLOYEES ONLY written in large font. Not sure whether this was the place, I called the number they'd given me. A husky voice answered the phone, and soon the door flung open. A middle-aged man with curly, wiry hair welcomed me with a smile. When I mentioned that the sign had confused me, he grabbed his belly and let out a hearty laugh.

"Then I guess the sign works. Please come in."

It was much larger inside than I'd imagined. The building had been remodeled so that each floor opened up to the middle of the building. The woody smell of sawdust pricked my nose. Handmade furniture was placed throughout the building, and people dressed in aprons were working on large slabs of timber. A group of people played pool in one corner of the building, and there was even someone lying on a sofa and listening to music. I studied each gathering of people as if they were the staffage of a large, intricate landscape painting. Even though the open office structure meant that everyone could see what you were doing, thanks to silly and eclectic pieces of art placed throughout the office, it didn't feel authoritarian.

The curly-haired man led me to a small room where he sat me down and offered me peppermint tea and a cookie that smelled of almonds. My gaze immediately drifted to the movie posters hanging on the wall behind him. Sensing my wandering gaze, he turned and pointed to one of the posters. He explained it was his favorite movie: *Born on the Fourth of July* starring Tom Cruise. It was one of my favorite movies, too, so I had no problem carrying on a conversation about how much of a classic it was. Before long, we were reminiscing about movies like *Far and Away* and *Rain Man* and lamenting the fact that Tom Cruise only seemed to do action movies these days. The conversation flowed naturally, but inside, I was a bit confused. Had I accidentally walked into the wrong interview?

"Forgive me, but—" I cautiously said, interrupting the conversation. "It's just that—Well, I'm afraid there may have been a misunderstanding. I thought I was here for a job interview."

Somewhat taken aback, the man hesitated before answering.

"This *is* your interview. In fact, you're the only person we decided to interview. I guess I got carried away talking about movies. I didn't even introduce myself. How rude of me."

He handed me his business card. Written under the company name "休 (sloth)"—which was a playful misreading of the character for "respite"—were the man's name and title written in a font that evoked the image of branches: Choi Jun-won, Lead Carpenter and CEO. Indeed, I'd applied to this company not knowing fully what they did here. Like most people looking for a new job, I had a habit of sending my personal statement and resume to whatever company was hiring. To make matters worse, their job posting had been uploaded under the cryptic title "Life-Creativity-Group."

From the small amount of research I'd done before the interview, I at least knew that they made furniture. I also knew from interviews I'd found online that their CEO had worked as a producer at an educational programming station before moving to Spain to study for a few years. And now, he was turning his love for woodwork into a business.

I'd once read that carpentry was a profession that would never disappear, no matter how much society progressed technologically. Machines of course would take on as much of the work as they could, but people who knew how to work with wood were irreplaceable.

Choi explained that his goal was to bring in talented carpenters and give them a friendly place to work. Although the company was new and hadn't quite figured everything out yet, at least its CEO had a clear vision for the company. And in line with that vision, he'd chosen the Chinese character *hyu* (休) for the name of the company—a character which meant "respite" and was a compound ideograph depicting a person resting in the shade of a tree. Hearing this, it occurred to me that this was just the kind of place that would foster creativity. There was only one problem. What did I know about working with wood?

"You see, I'm a romantic realist. That means I'm a realist with a bit of a romantic side."

He opened his arms magnanimously.

"That's why we are looking for someone who can give us practical inspiration."

"So that's why you're hiring me?"

He let out another hearty laugh. "Well, I haven't said you're hired. Not yet at least. I guess I should have been more upfront about that. Then again you *are* the only person we're interviewing. Anyway, I chose you because you're ordinary. Or more specifically, because you confessed in your personal statement that you're ordinary."

"I don't understand."

"Everyone here is a nutcase. It's hard to explain why, but it's true. Everything from the way we carry ourselves to the thoughts in our noggins is foolish and crazy. Most of us were working in other fields before we changed professions late in life to become carpenters. We're jagged rocks that don't fit in any hole, round or square, and we're always colliding with each other and mucking things up. We need someone to manage us. You might be ordinary out there. But in here? With all these nutcases? You'll be one of a kind. Everyone else who applied wrote about how great they were. You see, people have this tendency when writing personal statements to depict themselves as Indiana Jones or Superwoman. After a while, it felt like I was reading a book. What we need aren't novelists or Hollywood actors. What we need is someone mature and rational to manage us. In other words, someone who isn't a romantic realist, but a realistic romanticist."

"But I doubt I'm the only ordinary person in the world looking for a job. Don't take that the wrong way. I'm not trying to argue with you or say I don't want to work here."

"Of course there are others. That's why I wanted to meet you first before hiring you."

"And what do you think?"

He cleared his throat and then chuckled. "You know, I was really moved by your personal statement. I know it's not a writing competition, but you have a very calm and measured writing style. But now that I've met you, I realize you're no pushover either. Seeing the way you ask such direct questions. Being ordinary might be common, but it's also relative. There's extraordinariness even among ordinary people. From what I've seen, I think you and our team will get along well together."

And yet he still hadn't given me a definitive "You're hired." We continued talking for a while like friends, and eventually he explained the specifics of the contract. The salary was higher than I had expected. The way they cared so much about the welfare of employees, meticulously recording food expenses and overtime pay, really impressed me.

"Are you sure you can make a profit like this?"

Choi let out another long chuckle. "You know what I hate? The expression 'putting food on the table.' Of course, people have to put food on the table. You gotta eat to survive. But if that's all you care about, life becomes so dull. You gotta know how to have fun, too. That's the kind of company I want to run. Only time will tell if it's possible. So, Jihye, will you help me make this a reality?"

I'd never been asked a question like this during an interview. Could this be real?

"We've got all the hardware we need. And by hardware, I mean skilled workers who know how to cut and mend wood. What we need now is software. We need a program that teaches us how to make furniture that promotes happiness. To do that, we need a wholesome diet of art and literature. But I don't have the energy or time to think about such things. That's where you come in. Music, movies, books—we'll consume whatever you recommend for us. Your tastes will become the tastes of the company. Furniture made on such a wholesome diet of culture will, I hope, be at least a little better than furniture that's not."

Hearing this, my body started to shake with excitement. This interview made me dream. It made me wonder, *What if?*

"Are you sure there will be enough work for me here?" I asked as I clenched my sweaty palms.

He chuckled again. "An endless supply of it."

* * *

I agreed to start work at Sloth in two weeks, but I wasn't sure how to tell Team Leader Yu the news. After all, I'd only just become a regular employee, and now I was quitting? Not only that, but I felt a bit guilty because she'd recently opened up to me, sharing her personal opinions, on both life and work. I was trying to imagine the look on her face when she learned that I'd been sending out job applications while pretending to devote myself to this company. I waited for the right time to tell her, but with Kong Yun's sudden departure, the refunds we needed to issue her students, and Gyuok's untimely absences at work, I had to keep putting it off. And yet, I didn't want to stay here any longer than necessary. After Dept. Head Kim was fired, any faith I had in the company completely evaporated. If even *he* could be fired, what hope did I have for making a name for myself here? I knew I might regret it later, but my heart had already left the company. I had to leave.

The last ukulele class was held within those two weeks. The instructor said he was leaving the academy because he was busy with a new project. He scheduled a mini recital for our last class, in which each of us would perform a piece or two.

Instead of a banner or poster promoting the recital, all that was placed outside the classroom was a piece of printer paper with the words "Intermediate Ukulele 1 Recital" typed on it. Several employees from the academy, including Team Leader Yu, came to sit in on the performances, despite there not being much in the way of snacks and drinks.

And yet, there was something heartwarming about a little

recital in which people who hadn't known the first thing about performing on an instrument sat in front of an audience and showed that they could improve themselves.

Watching the others perform, I realized everyone had taken time out of their schedules to practice; they all played much better than when I'd last heard them in class.

Mr. Nam performed a ballad that was an arrangement of a popular K-pop girl group song, and it was quite beautiful. I knew that his teenage daughter usually found him embarrassing, but I had a feeling that, had she been there, she would have smiled with pride.

Stubbly-faced Muin, who I had assumed wouldn't come because he was busy preparing for that writing contest, went up stage and performed "Leopard of Mt. Kilimanjaro." He opened with a long and dramatic speech, and then began singing, working his way up to the climax while slowly adding more and more emotion until the end of the song, where he had to strain his voice and scream just to finish. The performance was more focused on the theatrics than it was on his technique and musicianship, but thanks to the cleaning ladies' warm reception, we were able to move on to the next performer without an awkward silence. The instructor commented on Muin's "experimental" performance with "I've never seen a ukulele performance quite like that"—a somewhat backhanded compliment. And yet, for some reason, Muin didn't smile. I'd never seen him look so serious and solemn before.

The elementary school student, whom the instructor once had such high hopes for during the spring semester, had shown little improvement since then. With a budding mustache of peach fuzz on his upper lip, he fought with his mother about going home before begrudgingly stomping up to the stage and giving a half-assed performance of another K-pop song. It was clear that he was embarrassed of his own voice, which had just started to drop with puberty. Thus the song, which was popular for its catchy hook, had been transformed into a monotone string of notes, as though he were chanting a Buddhist prayer. Once he was finished, the mother apologized to everyone and said that he'd just started puberty. He only proved her point with a grumpy "Stop it, Mom!"

Next, it was his mother's turn. She sat on stage and lifted her hand carefully up to the strings, her face flushed with nervousness. Everyone had expected the boy's to be the best performance, but to our surprise, it was his mother who'd made the biggest improvement. After performing a J. S. Bach cantata with emotion, good dynamic changes, and respectable intonation, she played an upbeat, rhythmic song titled "Guava Jam," for which she received the largest ovation of the recital. Even her son forgot his role as a sulking teenager, clapping the loudest for her. The instructor oohed and aahed before commenting that her performance gave him goose bumps. I remembered her saying that she'd given up on her dreams, but now her cheeks were glowing as though someone had lit a candle inside her. Her attire had changed too. She used to always dress in black, but today, she was wearing a pastel-colored knit with bright stripes and had her hair pulled back in a neat ponytail. I felt inspired, as well as guilty for having labeled her the "depressed" mom.

I was last on the program. I cleared my throat and began singing. It was a song I'd learned from Gyuok. I carefully plucked a harmony on the four strings and placed above it a quiet melody with my voice.

Missed the Saturday dance
Heard they crowded the floor

I was no Harry Connick Jr., but that didn't matter. I just sang it the only way I knew how. Early this year, I hadn't even known the difference between a ukulele and a miniguitar. I didn't know how to play an instrument, or how to make a beautiful sound. Until just a few months ago, Muin and Mr. Nam were complete strangers to me. But over that span of time, which felt both long and short to me, we'd shared stories, played foolish pranks on corrupt individuals, and learned how to play a few songs without looking down at our fingers. I wondered, though. Had I become wiser?

I didn't want the song to end because I was holding out for Gyuok to show up. He hadn't come to work today, and yet I hoped that he would stop by, just to listen to me sing. But he never came. When I finished, and after the audience left, the instructor spoke to us as if he'd just remembered something.

"If Gyuok had been here, I'm sure he would have given a wonderful performance. He may not be here with us today, but we can still listen to his song in our hearts. Please, a moment of silence for Gyuok."

No one objected to the instructor's bizarre proposal to turn the recital into a memorial service for a living man. As everyone closed their eyes, I wondered: What would Gyuok have sung had he been here? Perhaps a song of revolution? Or a love song? Or just a song without any lyrics, only whistling and humming. As I sat there in silence, I swore for a moment that I could hear in the distance the sound of his low, deep voice singing a faint tune.

18

EVERYONE!

There was an after-party following the recital, but only those who you'd expect to come came. The mother and her son went to their next cram-school lesson, and the instructor only showed his face for a moment at the restaurant before excusing himself. After he was gone, there were only three people left to go out for drinks: me, Muin, and Mr. Nam. At least, that is, until Gyuok appeared much later in the night. Clean-cut and wearing a suit, he looked unlike himself. It was obvious to me that he'd just come back from a job interview. I tried not to let our eyes meet, and yet that's exactly what happened several times, against my best efforts.

The mood that night was different. Conversations ended abruptly, and I kept having to rack my brain to think of new things to talk about. And because we were all too polite, none of us suggested calling it a night. Muin was the first to get drunk, and by a long shot. Ever since our graffiti adventure in Hongdae, he'd been hopeful and energetic, but tonight, his glossy eyes were filled with bitterness. He barely touched his food and just continued to knock back drink after drink. Only when his blood alcohol concentration reached its tipping point did he open his mouth and confess what was on his mind.

"I'm not going to write anymore. I've flirted with the idea many times before, but this time, it's for real. I'm not going to write any more screenplays. I'm going to look for a teaching position at an academy. I didn't submit my work to the competition. I knew I wouldn't win even if I did."

"You should send it in even if you don't think it will win. Writers gotta write, right?"

I wanted to encourage him because I knew that it'd taken a lot of courage to get himself out of that slump and pick up his pen again. But he didn't respond to me, and just pursed his lips as he took out his phone and handed it to us. A video was playing on the screen. It had been filmed at what looked like a recent movie premiere. A movie director and some A-list actors were on stage promoting the movie. Behind them was a large poster for an action movie. I'd seen videos like it before on TV and online.

Unable to wait for Muin to explain, Mr. Nam finally asked what was going on.

"It's mine," Muin mumbled.

"You've got to be more specific otherwise I can't understand you."

A bitter smile appeared on Muin's lips. "There was this screenplay competition two years ago. The prize pool was huge, and they promoted the crap out of it. I sent in one of my works. But on the day of the announcement, they said they'd failed to find a winner. And then a couple weeks ago, I saw the trailer for this movie. The plot is almost identical to mine."

"You didn't copyright it? There's a writers' guild, you know. It's not easy for people to get away with plagiarism these days."

"I did. A few months after submitting it to the competition. So I sent them a cease-and-desist letter. But they claimed they had their own copyright. It just so happens it was filed days before mine. But their screenplay was only three pages. Mine was one hundred! I couldn't believe it. I tried to convince myself that maybe it was just a coincidence. After all, it's hard to have an original idea these days. I tried to make myself forget about it. But then yesterday, I couldn't take it anymore. I went to the theatre to see for myself."

Muin paused and began to cry.

"It was identical to what I'd written. The dialogue, the plot, even the props were the same."

"Calm down, calm down. There must be another way."

"No, there isn't. Do you know who's behind that movie? DM. They own the biggest movie theatre chain in all of Korea. The fact that a giant corporation like DM is involved in this means only one thing: I'll never win."

I cleared my throat. This didn't just concern Muin. This was bigger than that.

"We can't let them get away with this," I said. "There's gotta be something we can do. Just because they're big doesn't mean they can just push us around. If you can't beat them in the courts, there's always forums and social media. There are so many channels through which we can protest and have our voices heard."

"You think protesting will change anything? Do I need to remind you of all the times protests have failed to make a difference? Even if I post evidence online, people will say they've heard it before. They'll claim the movie's different because the character names and tone have been changed. Or they'll tell me to get my revenge by making another, even more successful movie. But most likely they'll claim I'm just a no-name writer who's jealous because he's never been credited in a movie before. And if I try to publish my own screenplay, they'll slap me with a lawsuit of their own. That's the situation I'm in right now. I've been robbed blind with no way to prove it. It's like I don't exist."

People who don't exist. A bunch of nobodies. Something hot was working its way up from deep inside his chest. Right. We were nobodies because no one heard us when we screamed. We were no-bodies because we lived in semi-basement apartments. We were nobodies because we'd lost in the game of life. My chest ached. What had I been doing this whole time? Every moment I'd spent with these people, I'd been struggling to escape. I'd benefited from a cruel prank and become a regular employee, and now I was pre-paring to quit my job to work at another company. I had no right to be telling Muin what he should or shouldn't be doing. What would have happened had DM offered me a position at HQ? I would have taken their offer without hesitation. And then, I would never have needed to talk to these people again. And I would consider their failures not a matter of luck, but a matter of not trying hard enough, and nothing else. I realized I was a potential accomplice to the system that had exploited Muin. But this was my chance to be someone different.

"You have to say something. If you don't, they'll think they can get away with it. If you don't, they'll believe it's okay to steal from people."

My voice was growing. Me, who had lived for over a decade in the shadow of Kong Yun. I thought for a moment about how much courage it had taken to get out from underneath that woman. Muin and Mr. Nam looked as surprised at my forcefulness as I was.

"No, Muin's right. What difference will it make?" Mr. Nam said as he dropped his head. "You remember Congressman Han, don't you? He's doing as well as ever. I saw him on a morning talk show recently talking about the egging incident at the market. He just laughed it off as if it was nothing. And the hosts all took his side. They made us look like we were a nuisance to society. I didn't mention it to you guys, but when I saw him on TV like that, I felt so hopeless. I realized even my best efforts amounted to nothing."

"You don't know that," I said, not backing down. "If he has even an ounce of conscience left, I'm sure he reflected on what happened. And maybe he has a short-term memory and will start exploiting people again. But we can always give him a friendly reminder that injustice won't go unpunished. We might not be able to see the immediate effect of our actions, but we must keep showing the world that people aren't going to just stand by anymore."

We'd embarked on this mission with the resolve to change the world and ourselves. The time for pranks was over. Now, we needed to put up a real fight. In the past, we acted for the unspecified masses and did our best to stay under the radar. But it was time to unite.

As I explained this to them, the looks on their faces slowly turned from doubt to hope and solidarity.

But in the end, perhaps I should have been listening to the voice of doubt in my head. We were, after all, planning a suicide mission.

* * *

The movie was a commercial and critical success, breaking $5 million in ticket sales just a few days after opening at the box office. We discussed our plans for a while before we decided how we wanted to respond.

The schedule of promotional events for the movie was easily accessible from DM's home page. Because of this, we knew that, in just a few days, there would be a large stage greeting to commemorate the movie's surpassing $5 million in ticket sales at the largest theatre in Seoul. It was on that stage that we would make our move. Our goal wasn't to get the movie canceled. After all, innocent people had worked hard to make the movie. No, all we wanted was to scream from up on stage, where most people thought they couldn't go. But as the date approached, Muin stopped answering his phone.

"Does anyone know what Muin is doing these days?"

Mr. Nam continued to phone Muin, but he didn't pick up. Gyuok tilted his head in confusion. It was the eve of the attack, and we were starting to get worried that he'd never show up. But then late into the night he appeared at the bar. His face was pale. He stood there in silence for several seconds before finally speaking.

"I want you to stop."

But he wouldn't tell us why. All he said was that everything was his fault, and that he didn't want to make this any bigger than it had to be. His face was gloomier than I'd ever seen it.

"After all, nothing is going to change," he added hopelessly.

Gyuok took both of Muin's hands. "Just tell me one thing. Were you mistaken when you thought that they plagiarized your story?"

"No, that was the truth," Muin said with his head hanging low.

This reaffirmed the determination in Gyuok's eyes. "And yet, you've just decided that you want to lose the fight?"

"I can't explain it. All I know is that I can't do this. After all, it won't change anything."

Muin just repeated the same thing he'd already said, and then left. A gust of wind blew between us as he opened and closed the door.

"So, Muin doesn't want to do this," Mr. Nam said. "Does that mean we shouldn't either?"

"This isn't just for him," Gyuok said. "It's bigger than that. We're going. *I'm* going. Even if Muin doesn't come." None of us could deny the look in his eyes.

* * *

It passed like a dream. A dream I'd never dream again. It was the last time I'd ever be so innocent and naïve. It was quiet and brief. Like a mini silent film.

The stage was dark and empty and very large. The cast all went up wearing smiles, followed by the elderly director. He and the actors thanked the audience and bowed several times. The front row was filled with journalists holding cameras the size of small artillery. We were dispersed throughout the front row with them. And with every pass of the mic, we got tenser and tenser. Finally, one of the actors in the middle took the mic. He pledged to breakdance outside Gwanghwamun Gate if the movie broke $10 million ticket sales. Now was our time. We pulled out rodent masks, put them over our faces, and simultaneously stormed the stage. Gyuok and I took the stairs on the left; Mr. Nam took the ones to the right. Mr. Nam then snatched the mic from the actor as I held up a poster behind him. The poster demanded in thick red marker an apology from DM.

Mr. Nam started speaking in a halting voice. "Th—this movie—"

He suddenly froze, as though the size of the audience had finally got to him. There was no time for this. Gyuok stole the mic from him.

"This movie doesn't belong to DM. We are standing here today on behalf of our friend, the real owner of this movie, the one DM stole the idea from."

He passed the baton to me. My body felt like it was on fire. I had to be out of my mind.

"Everyone!"

That was the first and last thing the audience heard from me. I continued to scream into the mic, but the feed had already been cut off. Without the aid of the mic, my weak voice was like candlelight to the supernova of camera shutters below. The commotion was so loud, I couldn't even hear myself speak. Suddenly, my armpits itched, as though they were about to sprout wings. And then my feet started to float, as though I was taking flight. I looked over at Gyuok, who was cutting through the air. Even Mr. Nam seemed to be floating. We landed beneath the stage, bodyguards slamming us against the cold steps. Someone ripped off my mask. Suddenly, I was face-to-face with hundreds of people. Camera shutters erupted again. Today, for the first time in my life, I was the star of the show. But then I heard one of the supporting actors pick up the mic and say something. His witty statement would be used to teach scene-stealers for generations to come.

"I'm sorry about that. This was all set up to promote the movie. Unfortunately, it didn't go quite as planned. Next time, we'll make sure we practice more beforehand. Thank you."

I'd never been so famous. For the next six hours "masked vigilantes crash movie promotion" trended number one on the internet, and after the better part of a day, all our identities were leaked online. But our newfound fame lasted for less than two days, as the world had more important news to be reported. And with that, we were cast to the side, like a trio of over-the-hill actors.

19

FARAWAY STRANGER

We were released near dawn. But before that, two people—a representative from the movie studio and a public relations officer from DM—were sent to speak with us. They exchanged humorous looks when they learned that both Gyuok and I worked for a subsidiary of DM. They questioned us more than anything, and before leaving said they would be seeing us again to take care of some "administrative matters."

Prison food tasted like garbage. And unlike the Korean idioms that suggested otherwise, the rice did *not* in fact contain beans like I'd expected. Even the spinach, which had been reboiled so many times it disintegrated at the touch of a spoon, was saltier than seawater. Thankfully, we only spent one night in the holding cell. As the police opened the doors for us, they clicked their tongues and said we were wasting our lives. When Mr. Nam heard this, he very nearly charged at them. Thankfully, Gyuok managed to hold him back, preventing us from getting into more trouble.

Out on the street, we were greeted by the pale blue of dawn.

Depending on how you looked at it, these could either be the last seconds of night or the first of a new day. No one spoke a word, at least until Mr. Nam broke the silence with an agreeable suggestion.

"How about some hangover soup?"

We hunched over our bowls in silence and seasoned our soup with dried radish and congealed blood. Usually, we'd order drinks, too, but no one suggested doing so. We were all, it seemed, aware that it was over. But perhaps the end had been foreshadowed two days ago, the moment Muin walked out on us. On the TV set hanging from the wall in the restaurant was a food-and-travel show featuring the recent "morning jogging" fad that was sweeping across Korea. We changed the channel and found a news report about the hit movie from DM Studios that was breaking records. On the screen, the cast and director were bowing to an audience of reporters. Then, without even a change in tone, the news anchor reported that a group of masked men and women appeared, crashing the event. What followed was a shaky cell phone video of our blurred-out faces. Looking at it from afar like this, I realized that the protest was much shorter and more pointless than I'd even imagined.

"I guess we finally made the news," Mr. Nam said sarcastically.

I glanced toward Gyuok. He had his head down and seemed to be thinking about something. Suddenly, the image on the TV changed to footage of a man.

"Hey, that's—" Mr. Nam shouted.

It was Muin. He had a baseball cap pulled over his eyes, but we could tell it was him. He was speaking to the camera as though making an emotionless apology.

"I think there's been a misunderstanding—"

The news channel only showed this short clip before silencing

Muin's audio; they summarized the rest of his interview themselves.

"The controversial writer emphasized that DM Studios did *not* plagiarize his work, and that any similarities between the movie and his screenplay are simply a matter of coincidence. He apologized for the actions of the masked men and women, whom he claims he barely knows."

The news report ended with another video of the cast greeting a swarm of fans and journalists with smiles. We sat on the floor and ate cold hangover soup as we looked up helplessly at people on TV, as though we were nothing but faraway strangers observing beings from another planet.

* * *

Jihwan's hands were in his pockets as he tapped the floor with his foot. Standing behind him were Mom and Dad. Now they'd seen for themselves the semi-basement apartment their daughter was living in, and yet they still had nothing to say. Mom quickly prepared dinner, and when she was done, the four of us huddled around the table, in a cramped room that never got any sunlight. I realized it'd been years since we'd eaten together like this. But I was incapable of lifting my head to take the moment in because I was ashamed that my poor living conditions were the reason for our reunion. I slowly reached for my chopsticks when the lint-colored square of tofu in the middle of the table caught my eye. And as I looked at it, tears formed in my eyes as a confused laugh simultaneously broke the silence in my throat. Unable to take it any longer, my father told me to stop sulking and eat.

Few words were exchanged that night. Once they were gone,

I glanced around my room at all the pears and apples; it felt like they'd brought a whole orchard and left it in my room. A house-warming present of sorts. I felt wrong that I was eating the hard-earned fruits of my parents' labor when I'd failed to produce any such fruit myself.

I called Choi at Sloth and told him I couldn't take the job. He asked why, and I just sent him a link to the video of my stunt at the movie theatre.

—I guess I'm a bit of a nutcase, too.

He'd read the message but never replied. A while later, I got a text message, just not from Choi.

—I have something I need to say to everyone.

It was Muin.

* * *

Our last meeting occurred in the bar where we'd had our first. Everyone looked gloomy, as if waiting for the final curtain. Muin arrived a bit later than promised. He looked the same yet different somehow. His facial expressions, his aura—it was as if he belonged to a different world. He was now a stranger to us. No sooner did Muin sit down than he picked up a beer and started drinking.

"How could you do such a thing?" Mr. Nam asked. "I've read truly hateful comments on my mukbang videos before, but never have I been as hurt as I am now. I feel like a marionette at a third-rate puppet show: I feel like I've been played."

Suddenly, a terrifying heat surrounded us. I wanted to stay calm. But then I realized, I had no reason to be worried; my heart was already ice-cold. I didn't touch my beer. Alcohol was for celebrating or grieving, and this was neither.

"We deserve an explanation," I said as I crossed my arms in front of my chest.

Muin swallowed hard. "I was very clear. I told you all not to do it. I knew nothing would change. You guys acted on your own, against my wishes. And how'd that turn out for you?"

He was trying to sound tough, but I could hear a nervous tremor in his voice. It was hard to stare at his face for too long, out of fear of what might happen. But not Gyuok. He was looking Muin right in the eye. He chugged his beer and sneered.

"It was money—" Gyuok mumbled.

"What'd you say?" Muin asked, suddenly lifting his head.

"They paid you, didn't they? I met with someone from the studio today. They handed me a document and asked me to sign it. When I asked them what was going on, they explained that they'd already settled with you. Just before the incident at the movie theatre. It sounded too cliché to be true. But I guess it wasn't. Sad."

Muin cocked his head to the side and let out a soulless laugh. I just noticed it, but he was wearing a T-shirt with Che Guevara's face printed on it. Gyuok seemed to have noticed this, too.

"You're wearing a Che Guevara T-shirt, but you don't even know what he did," Gyuok said, his eyes refusing to blink. "You sold your work to the people who stole it from you for pennies on the dollar, and then lied to us about it. Coward."

Muin jumped to his feet.

"Yeah? Well, you better watch what you say. The only reason you can say that is because you've never experienced hunger." Muin's tone was becoming aggressive. "I jumped into this like, 'What the hell.' I was having fun and doing something meaningful. That's all that mattered. But then one day I looked in my bank account and realized I didn't even have enough to cover my cell phone bill. That woke me up, all right. But there was something I couldn't figure out. Why am I struggling while you have so much time on your hands, Gyuok? How do you have the time to kick back and judge people all day? So I did some digging. About you. And you know what I found? Your father's a professor of doctors at a large hospital, and your house . . . Well, let's just say it's the kind of house average people like us could never buy even if we saved up our whole life. I don't care if you think I'm petty for it. I wanted to throw up when I realized who you really are. You're not like us. You've got all the money in the world."

When Muin was done, he took a big gulp of the saliva that had pooled inside his mouth.

Gyuok shook his head in disbelief. "You're arguing guilt by association. What my father does has nothing to do with me. And just because I came from money doesn't mean I can't—"

"Nothing to do with you? Do you know how much I've suffered? How many times I've gotten rejected and used? Do you know what it's like to constantly worry about putting food on the table? I thought it was just because I was powerless. Every day, I vowed to myself that when I finally made it, I would stick it to all the people who laughed at me. My old friends used to blame the system that was skewed toward others, they cursed capitalism and the injustices of the world. Up to that point, we were all comrades. But people change so easily at the sight of money. I always wondered why that was, and then one day I figured it out. Getting close to victory is hard. That's the world we live in. No matter what happens this time, in the end, the results are the same. What do you know about our world?"

Muin was practically screaming now. And he wasn't finished.

"You think you're all that, but you have no right to judge others or incite them. We're here struggling and fighting for food, while you were born with a silver spoon in your mouth. And yet you talk about revolution and fighting against authority. It makes me sick. Of course, you'll never get it. You've just experienced it once like going on a field trip to the factory. When the time is right, you'll realize this isn't for you and you'll go back to your comfortable life. You're nothing. You're just a fake."

Muin was talking so forcefully that he stumbled and fell to the ground.

"So that's how it is?" Gyuok said as he got out of his chair.

What was said next should never have been said, things that you just don't say to someone you once considered your comrade. And the looks they gave each other were saying that deep down, they were fundamentally different people, that they could never see eye to eye. They spat insults meant to cause great pain and injury.

When I came to, I was already on my way home. I guess you didn't always need alcohol to feel drunk. Everything felt like a dream; I couldn't remember what was said toward the end, who threw the first punch, or how everyone left. My legs were shaking, and there was the thin rattle of metal in my ears.

I lost myself in the crowds and yet somehow managed to find my way back to my apartment.

"I need to find a new home."

While it was true that my lease was up next month, it was more than that. I didn't want to associate with those three anymore. I wanted to retreat inside myself. I wanted to live just for me. To hell with the rest of the world.

And yet, I couldn't make any judgment regarding Gyuok. I felt a stabbing pain in my chest when I thought about our short kiss. *There was nothing between us.* I repeated these words to myself one syllable at a time. *There was nothing between us.* But this wasn't enough. I opened the notes folder on my cell phone and typed out a message for myself. When I went over the message to fix the spaces I'd missed, my fingers instinctively placed periods between the words.

THERE. WAS. NOTHING. BETWEEN. US.

For a brief moment, I almost convinced myself that it was true. But the pain. Not the wound of unrequited love, but a complex feeling of torment. Or perhaps it was the feeling of guilt I'd tried to hide. A sense of guilt that culminated on the night when I chose to stop kissing Gyuok. In my mind, I'd told him no matter how much I liked him, I couldn't spend my future with him—a petty defense mechanism put up by my vanity. All the while, I'd been unable to express my reservations about associating with him. In the end, Muin was the mirror that showed me my true feelings.

Perhaps I knew this all along. That these acts couldn't change the world, that they couldn't break anyone or anything. I just couldn't say it out loud. I was too much of a coward to show the shallowness of my sincerity. In some way, Muin had been more honest than I was. He had owned up to the truth that I had ignored.

The phone rang and rang. I didn't pick up. Could it be who I thought
it was? Or was it someone else? Both possibilities terrified me. Just
as the phone seemed like it would stop ringing, someone appeared
before me. It was Gyuok, gaunt and scruffy. His fair skin had turned
pale, and his pupils sparkled blue. Even though he looked like he
hadn't showered, I could smell the scent of fabric softener coming
from him. Right. Once upon a time, I'd liked this. The contradictions
of his appearance. The way he smelled of freshly laundered clothes,
despite looking like he never went shopping, and the incongruity
between his disheveled hair and immaculate skin. His cheeks were
a bit pink, however, as though he'd been drinking.

"I need to know what you really think." Gyuok's body swayed as
he spoke. "Do you truly think I'm a fake?"

I looked straight at him, at his innocent eyes, at his candid expression, at that chest and those hands which had once held me
and given me so much courage.

"No." I paused before continuing. "It's just that I can't stay in
your world."

Gyuok let out a laugh. When I saw that smile, the way his shoulders moved up and down despite the fact nothing I said was funny,
I became afraid, afraid that I might start to like him even more, that
I might fall dangerously into a preposterous world, that I might
be filled with regret. But it was Gyuok who said something unexpected.

"I just want to tell you in case you thought otherwise. I love
you. So very much."

"What?"

This was the wrong confession. And yet I was too dazed to do
anything for a moment, but then asked why.

"Why?" Gyuok smiled. "Because you're beautiful."

The air entering and exiting my lungs froze.

"Everything you do is beautiful. You act so tough all the time, but I know that deep down, you're warm and gentle. And most importantly, you're honest. You don't realize it, but every gesture you make, every word you speak, every look you make with your eyes, shows your true feelings."

I shook my head furiously. I made a scoffing sound as moisture filled my eyes. If this were any other day, if this had been that night in his apartment, perhaps I would have felt different. But now, this confession was too hard to listen to. Angry at him for his horrible timing, I let the tears in my eyes go.

"I've been thinking a lot since Dept. Head Kim quit," he continued, his speech fast and jittery. "I started to doubt whether what we were doing was really just pranks. It might be futile, but I wanted to dig deeper and get to the heart of the matter. I've become a fundamentally different person. Of course, it will take time for these changes to take effect, but I had to tell you. I had to tell you because—"

"No, don't. Please," I said, cutting him off. "I have something I need to tell *you*. Something I'm embarrassed of. I'm no different than Muin. I'm not courageous. I pretended to associate with you guys because I wanted to forget the truth, because I wanted to be cool, because I hated being alone. But deep down, I doubted everything, and that made me feel like a giant hypocrite. I was terrified I would be found out. And now that I've told you the truth, even though it is a bit late, I feel better. I want to work on myself. I want to stop worrying about other people. So please, please. Don't get in my way."

Silence fell between us. Gyuok turned his body slowly and made a gap for me, through which I escaped. I started walking faster and faster, because I wanted to put the embarrassing memories I'd shared with him and the others behind me. I pushed on the ground with all my strength, sending the earth and everything between him and me back into the vanishing past.

That day, something changed. A final curtain had been drawn. I'd experienced ends many times in my life, but never one with such finality. I'd call this ending "bitter," but that wouldn't quite do it justice. And just like that, our adventures—which could only be described as a slight disturbance in the grand order of things— ended.

* * *

Sometimes you must quit, even when you already have nothing. Sometimes, you must erase everything and take the time to withdraw into yourself. There might be people who say you're just young and being immature. But whatever. I needed time to be alone. Not just to eat and watch movies, but to be truly alone. The only excuse I can give you is that "We all experience a time like that in our lives at least once." I'm not sure who said that, but that's exactly how I felt right then.

On Monday, I told Team Leader Yu I was quitting. She reached out and put her hand on my shoulder but said nothing. It looked as though she already knew everything. I entered this company against stiff competition and worked for months to become a regular employee, but now I was ending it all with just a few words and a single piece of paper. But that is often the case with endings.

Easy, fast, and unexpected. And sometimes, they come at exactly the right time.

I didn't see Gyuok. Team Leader Yu told me to say goodbye to him before I left, but I ignored her wishes.

Before leaving the office, I looked back at my empty chair. I imagined who would take my place when I was gone. Whoever it would be, that chair didn't belong to me anymore. The moment I stepped out those doors, I would forever lose any way of proving that it had ever been mine.

The view from the street was the same as ever. No one cared that I'd done something socially unacceptable or that I'd spent a night in jail. But I was grateful for my insignificance, which owed a great debt to the horrifying, tragic, and sensational events of the world. Soon forgotten were the struggles of people too ordinary to attract people's attention.

I boarded a bus. A familiar tune was playing on the radio. It was "The Blue Room," but not the one Gyuok had played for me in his apartment. This one was being performed by the Hamilton Sisters. This rendition's upbeat tempo and optimistic naivete was a painful reminder that the hushed emotions exchanged that night had all but evaporated.

* * *

Team Leader Yu gave me a small present the day I went to the office to collect my things. Smiling up at me from my palm was a rosy-cheeked girl in blue—a lucky Russian doll. Team Leader Yu said she'd bought it as a souvenir while traveling in Russia, back before getting married.

"But why are you giving it to me?"

"I guess you've grown on me. I wanted to wish you good luck. In time, you'll learn that we all have people of different sizes and colors stored deep inside the layers of our hearts."

I gently curled my hand around hers.

"In that case, I have something I want to show you. Call it a confession?"

I led her outside the academy to my secret hiding place. A gust of wind sent the dry fallen leaves spinning in tight ringlets on the ground. I pointed to the bench at one end of the park.

"Meet Mr. Jeong-jin."

Team Leader Yu glanced around in confusion.

"I can't see anybody."

"Only people pure of heart can," I said playfully.

The stunned look on Team Leader Yu's face slowly turned into a smile.

"I hope you don't think I was going to pretend like I could see him. I'm not that stupid."

We both laughed. I then told her the truth about Mr. Jeong-jin's origin. "I never knew," she said before nodding slightly. This was the first time we'd ever understood each other, and it only took saying goodbye for it to happen.

20
EMPTY CHAPTER

By now, my time at Diamant Academy had become nothing more than a memorable episode. Back when I worked there, each day had felt like an eternity, but now that I was gone, it was just a thing of the past, a period in my life I could refer to simply with the words "back then."

For a while after leaving the company, my life was uneventful. Were I to ever publish my autobiography, that chapter would be nothing but a blank page. And yet, it would be a chapter that I would argue vehemently with my editor to keep.

I continued to exchange a text here and there with Mr. Nam, but that only lasted for a short while. The last I'd heard was that he'd opened his own Udon restaurant somewhere in Seoul. I was glad he was making customers happy with his cooking instead of filming himself eating for the entertainment of others.

Muin's whereabouts were a mystery to me until one day I stumbled across a webtoon of his. It had caught my eye with its unique title: *The Rubber Man Strikes Back*. I was immediately reminded of how he said his favorite movie was *The Last Rubber Man*. He was neither a success story nor a failure. He was simply living his life day by day, persistent and honest. It was a life I didn't dare judge. I wished that he would continue to live that way.

As for Kong Yun, her new book eventually came out, but it wasn't the same resounding success that her first book had been. After getting married, she became famous again though, this time as a power blogger. Makeup reviews, name-brand bags, hotel food, international travel—her blog had it all. Of course, there was no way of telling whether her life was truly as glamorous as she portrayed it to be. But if there was one thing I knew, it was that she had no influence over me anymore.

After turning down the job at Sloth, I worked on my portfolio for a while before sending out my resume again. The company that eventually hired me was the same one I'd turned down to become unemployed.

When Choi recognized me at the interview, he looked happy to see me again.

"You know, even the most ordinary people are nutcases when you look close enough. I guess it's fate that we would work together."

Gene editing, 3D printers, drones—there was talk that we were at the beginning of a Fourth Industrial Revolution, and yet here were a group of carpenters attempting to start a business with nothing but sweat, muscle, and good old human creativity. They made everything from baby cribs to desk stands, and it was all beautiful and unique. Just as Choi had intended, I contributed to the company by studying recent trends and feeding the employees with a healthy diet of art and culture.

Sloth went through a few crises but had now stabilized and was starting to expand. Choi even recruited craftspeople from other fields outside of carpentry. As far as he was concerned, anything made by hand could become fine art with enough skill and artistry.

So there I was, a thirty-two-year-old project manager in charge of three other employees. I always had a mountain of work on my desk, just as the case had been at Diamant, and I still didn't have the time to put a personal touch on any work that I only got paid a fixed salary for. My life had become a vicious cycle of work, sleep deprivation, caffeine, and yet more sleep deprivation. It was sad to think that my only motivation for working was a monthly paycheck, but that was life.

Sometimes, when I was exhausted or feeling down, I would take out my ukulele and pluck a few tunes. You'd be surprised at just how comforting four nylon strings and a box of wood can be. My fingers still remembered the notes from that piece of music I performed in front of everyone. And whenever I sang that song, I always pictured the same face. And when that happened, questions tormented my mind like unfinished homework.

The last news I'd heard regarding Gyuok was that he'd been hired at some company. I was relieved that his life had regained some stability, but my chest still ached whenever I thought about him. Changing the world through games and pranks. Had it ever been possible? What had Gyuok truly intended to accomplish? Perhaps he was just trying to release his suppressed ego, like a child acting out. But I had to stop myself from asking these questions before it was too late. That was the only way I could protect my convalescent heart.

Just as Jihwan said, the most practical way to go through life wasn't to try to change the world but to walk safely along a designated path. And yet for some reason, I still didn't want to do that. Whenever I reminisced about those failed pranks, my chest was seized by a whirlwind of emotions that escaped expression. When enough time had passed, I gained the ability to diagnosis my ailment. I was suffering from the desire to incite my own change in the world. The only problem was that the question of how exactly I wanted to do that kept evading me, as though its answer was always just on the tip of my tongue.

And then one day, I came to a vague realization: Mr. Jeong-jin might know.

* * *

It'd been some time since I'd moved out of my old neighborhood and that old semi-basement apartment. And yet when riding the bus, I would sometimes pass by Diamant Academy, or what used to be Diamant Academy. Indeed, it had been demolished not long after I left. The last time I'd seen the building, large bulldozers were smashing holes in its concrete. And lying on the ground, surrounded by gnarled rebar in the rubble, was the scrap metal and broken glass of what had once been a dazzling company sign. Having decided that its ivory tower of education was a waste of money, DM had bought up all the real estate in the area to build a fortress more in line with its identity and profit goals. Having never seen the inside of the new complex, I got off the bus to have a look around.

A movie theatre, shopping mall, yuppie coffee shops, and what seemed like every franchise in existence. It was what we referred to as a "complex culture space," a sort of one-stop shop for all your "culture" needs—if by culture, you meant the kind of large-scale, easily accessible, feel-good culture that turned a profit. The space was packed with shoppers strutting about gleefully. But I wondered, was a shopping center really the answer? After just a few minutes, I became claustrophobic from the way every inch of space seemed to have been made with a cookie cutter. I couldn't believe this was the ground on which I'd once worked. There was no trace of me anywhere.

It was then that I realized I wanted to see an old friend. I crossed the street and entered a familiar alley. Everything in the neighborhood had changed except for the quiet space inside this apartment complex. Here, even the joggers and amphitheatre were just as I remembered them. I walked over to my old bench and sat down.

"Hello, Mr. Jeong-jin," I whispered, hoping no one would hear me and think I was crazy. "Have you been well?"

I felt a strange warmth spread through my chest. I took my time and remained on the bench until the sun began to set. I had initially thought that this park was just as I had left it, but when I looked more closely, I noticed there were a few murals on the walls, and someone had weeded the stairs and the planters. And yet, it was still just a space doing nothing. It was then that I got the inspiration to plan an event.

It took three months to prepare for it. At first, I didn't mention it to anyone I knew because I was too embarrassed that they might laugh at me. But just before I finalized everything, I decided to send out an invitation. And as I did this, somewhere far away, a disturbance was stirring.

21

RAINBOW

The news lately was abuzz with stories of corruption surrounding the Chaebols of Korea. Stock manipulation, collusion, political bribes—it seemed like there was no end to the rabbit hole of corporate greed. It all began with a tip from an anonymous informant—or informants—who had previously been employed at one branch of a large family tree of conglomerates, one of which just happened to be DM.

Indeed, no one knew if the informant was one person working alone or a coordinated group. Whatever the case, it seemed like he, she, or they had gotten employed for the sole purpose of uncovering the truth, going the hard route of being hired as an intern and slowly working their way up to a position as an executive secretary or personal accountant.

For months, they'd been leaking information to a progressive news outlet that in turn did the journalistic legwork to fact-check everything. According to one news report I saw, the whistleblower had been instrumental in providing the government hearing with a long list of witnesses who could be summoned and questioned. The informant declined an official interview or to reveal their identity, and simply chose to spread a message, read on the evening news for the entire country to hear.

"The world may never change, but sometime in the future, when we are old and close to death, we will remember this day. All I hope is that when that day comes, we will still be capable of criticizing the injustices of the world, just like we are capable of doing right now."

The anchor then paused, explaining that he didn't know what the last bit meant:

"Everyone! Wherever you are sitting, whatever authority you may or may not have, remember this: A chair is just a chair!"

These last words entered my ear like a key fitting into its lock. It felt like a secret code that only I knew, a message dispatched to me from a distant land.

* * *

People trickled into the circular park. To those who didn't know, we probably looked like local residents or even vagabonds. Once there were enough people, they started taking their seats in front of the amphitheatre's steps, with food and drink in hand. A little while later, several people dressed in black tights and paint took to the stage and started moving their bodies. A form of shadow puppetry. The audience lost itself in the imagery of black silhouettes dancing against the backdrop of the setting sun. The play didn't last long, and soon, the stage was empty again. Suddenly, a man jumped up on stage and sang a love song. He needed more practice, but the audience politely clapped for him when he was finished.

Placed in front of the stage was a small sign. "Everyone is welcome on stage. Have the courage to jump!" An open mic of sorts. To prepare for this event, I scouted out several do-nothing spaces in Seoul, went to the local bureau every day to persuade skeptical government employees, and raised a small amount of money for the event through crowdfunding.

People were free to go up on stage and do whatever they wanted. Sing, dance, tell a story. There was no line dividing the audience from the stage. Round holes in a square city. That was the idea behind this event. I wanted to tear down walls and transform an otherwise meaningless lot into a space where everyone had the chance to participate. I wanted to create stages like this throughout Seoul. Today was just the first of many.

I'd been worried that people would be too shy to participate, but to my pleasant surprise the oncoming night seemed to give them courage.

Just as the sun began to paint the sky a brilliant orangey red, I saw him. A man leaning against a streetlamp in the distance. Dusk had made him nothing but a dark shadow, but I could tell he was looking at me. Suddenly, the cries of cicadas rushed into my ears from the air above my head like a towering wave of water. In the short moment that I opened my mouth and turned my gaze up to the sky, he had disappeared from underneath the streetlamp. He was walking toward me now.

"How are you?" Gyuok asked, as though we were meeting each other for the first time.

He'd lost a lot of weight, but his eyes were clear and lucid.

"Good. And you?"

"I came because I was curious what you've been up to. I heard rumors that you've been reusing old material. Mr. Jeong-jin, again?"

Gyuok pointed to what was written on the pamphlet.

JEONGMAL, JINJJA, WOORI
TRULY, REALLY, US

It was the name I'd given this theatre, and it was also my inside joke. It appeared that Gyuok had finally figured out the origin of Mr. Jeong-jin's name.

I chuckled. "I wanted to try something a little different. Here, anyone can go up on stage and participate. There are no designated seats here. No chairs, only stage."

"Ah-ha. Those infamous chairs." Gyuok brought his hand up to his forehead.

"I hate what people say about these do-nothing spaces. That they need to be repurposed and developed. Do-nothing spaces are perfect for just that: doing nothing and having fun. And until now, I've kept Mr. Jeong-jin all to myself. I decided it was time that I gave him back to everyone."

"Give him back, you say? Creating something from nothing. Sounds courageous."

Gyuok's shoulders shook up and down as he laughed. As he did this, his protruding Adam's apple movement moved in unison with his body. His laugh hadn't changed one bit.

"What have you been up to?" I asked.

"Me? I lost everything. But it was part of an experiment to see if I could really do it. In that sense, I guess I succeeded. Call me bankrupt if you want. Although, I'm not sure if you'll believe me."

"You haven't changed a lot."

"I haven't had much of a chance. Not yet at least."

He said this as if there was more to explain, then handed me his company business card.

"It was hard getting hired again. I concluded that if there was something that needed to change, I first needed to learn, and let it be known, what it was that needed to be changed. And now that I've started, I want to see it through to the end. I want to know if I still can't change, even after all that."

"And are you going to give up those pranks?"

"I'm not sure. Should I?"

Gyuok snorted a laugh before walking down the steps and up to the stage. In his arms was an instrument I'd seen many times before. A soft melody tickled my ears. The song had returned to me after a long time, as if someone had placed a repeat sign at the very end of a long piece of music. It was the song he'd once played before me, the song I'd once performed for him.

Some people paid attention to his performance while others chatted among themselves quietly. I could hear the hum of cars passing by. There was something commonplace about this scene, an evening concert in late summer. Car engines, cicadas, a lonely ukulele—these sounds melted together, causing the space to pulsate like a giant fetus.

We made eye contact. A smile started to form on his lips. I raised my eyebrows slightly for him. I felt something warm and private being exchanged between us. This is what it felt like to find a comrade, someone of like-mindedness. The smiles on our lips spread to the rest of our faces, and eventually morphed into sound. An eternal song had just begun. After several minutes of showering the earth with its last fiery energy, the sun had all but disappeared, surrendering the sky and Seoul to the darkness of the night.

* * *

Many months ago, back when I just couldn't seem to catch a break, I'd come outside after failing at yet another job interview—this one for a position that seemed tailored just for me—and was met by blindingly bright day. .Actually the weather was cloudy, not a blank patch of sky to be seen, and yet for some reason, I couldn't open my eyes when looking up at the sky. It hadn't rained recently, but the ground was wet as far as I could see. It was surreal and didn't make sense to me.

I trudged through the streets before a rainbow on the ground stopped me in my tracks. An oil slick was floating in a puddle, producing a brilliant display of colors. The hues and lines were so clear and vivid that it looked more real to me than any rainbow I'd ever seen. It was so beautiful and peculiar that I couldn't help myself and stood there, staring at it for what felt like minutes. It then occurred to me that not all rainbows are bound to clear skies after rainfall. Beautiful rainbows can exist anywhere. Most people's fondest memories are the product of interesting characters and outlandish events. But as for me, I'll never forget that oil slick on the ground.

I might only be a speck of dust in the universe, but there's always the possibility that I might land somewhere and catch the light just right so that I become a beautiful rainbow. If that happens, I'll be the only one of my kind in the universe, without ever having screamed at the top of my lungs, claiming that I'm someone special. It took a lot of time and effort before I realized that, but there's this small twist: even had I not tried that hard, it would have always been true.

A NOTE FROM THE AUTHOR

Somehow I've published two books in half as many years. If you'd told me a year ago that I'd be not only a published author, but one with two books to her name, I'd have called you crazy. I wrote the first draft of this novel in February and March of 2015. Other matters required my attention after finishing it, so the manuscript remained unused for a while, but now, on the year Jihye would have turned twenty-nine, the book has finally come alive. *Ordinary Person* was the title of the first manuscript, *Born 1988* was the title of the version that won the award, and *Counterattacks at Thirty* was, of course, the title that got officially published. It's a dynamic title, but I can't help but worry. If someone were to ask me right now if I had some piece of advice, some words of wisdom for the generation about to enter their thirties, I'd say: "Not really." They're sick and tired of advice and wisdom, and I have no intention of adding to their angst.

Once upon a time, I thought I had talent. That was back when I used to get compliments for barely trying. And yet, I could never reach the place I wanted to reach. Just when I thought I was almost

there, a tall mountain would appear before me. I would exert myself to summit the mountain only to be confronted by a cliff. It was
the type of journey that would make anyone want to throw their
hands up in defeat. All my hard work, all my *colors*, were tossed
aside with ridicule. And then I'd receive the heartless advice to start
over, from absolute zero, without any hints or guidance about how
to move forward. And if I couldn't do it? Then I should just quit.
These were the orders given to me by judges I had never, would
never, meet. Orders from "above."

I found comfort in pitying those people, the critics who told me
to "start over." I told myself that these nameless judges who knew
nothing about me had missed something precious in my work, thus
preventing that precious something from being born into the world.
I laughed, put up a front, vowed never to give up. It was my own
form of counterattack, so to speak. But it didn't matter; whether
I practiced this vain form of pity or cried out in exhaustion, the
world didn't care. But all of this was a blessing in disguise. It taught
me that reaching great heights is difficult and that my repeated failures were also the failure of others.

While writing this novel, I would sometimes look up from my
computer and study the young people in the café. They'd be taking
mock exams or practicing interviews in groups, their faces tired
and expressionless. Holding onto a dream that may or may not
come to pass, they put their heads down and charged ahead, de-
termined to give it their all. In that sense, they were not different
from me; I could refer to us as "we." Tasteful music would fill the
air like the smell of coffee. And sweet romantic songs massaged
the heart. (That's one reason I chose several upbeat jazz songs to
serve as the soundtrack for this novel.) And as I looked at them, I

wanted to ask: What kind of adult do you want to become? How are you going to remember the present moment, how are you going to etch it into your memory? Even if you're not convinced of the efficacy of counterattacks, shouldn't we all live our lives with at least a little bit of rebelliousness? This book is the amalgamation of these questions and ideas.

I still remember the nights when I would walk home from the café after working on this book, smelling the crisp air with faint hints of spring. I also remember the excitement I felt the day I finished the novel. What kept me writing was the unwavering support of my family despite my unpromising future, and the smiles of my baby, who seemed oblivious to the war raging inside her mother's bosom.

Receiving the Jeju 4•3 Peace Literature Award made me feel a range of complicated emotions, including slight embarrassment. The time between receiving the award and the book's publishing had been a humbling process, one that allowed me to remember what I was like two and a half years ago and to retrace the internal journey I've taken since then.

For my next work, I have resolved to write a work that can reach the hearts of many, that will find people where they are, somehow, some way. The kind of resolution that I'm afraid I might break. But I've taken this fear hostage, and I won't let it go until I've succeeded.

Won-pyung Sohn
Fall 2017

A NOTE ON THE TRANSLATION

Readers will be forgiven for thinking that two different authors wrote *Almond* and *Counterattacks at Thirty* (hereafter *C.A.T.*). Whereas *Almond* is a beautifully simplistic work of young adult fiction about a neurodivergent boy who struggles to feel emotions, *C.A.T.* is a wonderfully ambitious novel about an ordinary yet jaded woman in her thirties who has been struggling her whole life to stand out from the crowd. The books also vary widely in what they demand from a reader in terms of knowledge about contemporary South Korean society. And while technically the two books have been translated by two different people, Sandy Joosun Lee and I have worked hard to stay true to the essence of each respective text. Indeed, about the only thing the two works have in common is their masterful craftsmanship. But why should an author's first and second novel be alike? While Sohn has every right to attempt to recreate the success of a hit like *Almond*, her ability to achieve the same—if not greater—level of sophistication with a novel completely different from her first book in subject matter, character, and writing style puts her in league with South Korea's best story-tellers.

One particularly noteworthy difference between the two books is their titles, both of which were translated more or less literally into English. *Almond*'s title needs no further explanation once the reader understands that it refers to the main character's underdeveloped almond-shaped amygdala. But what about *Counterattacks at Thirty*? "Thirty" of course refers to the Korean age of the narrator,* but "counterattacks" is not as straightforward. Indeed, while I'm no expert in thinking up catchy titles, I have a suspicion that the word "counterattacks" (*bangyeok* in Korean) will leave many readers in a state of vaguely puzzled anticipation, like someone waiting for an explanation to a familiar term used in an unfamiliar context. While the events of the novel somewhat elucidate the title's meaning, the text avoids spelling out all of its nuances for readers. In fact, the word "counterattack" only appears in the original text three times, one less time in the English version because "counterattack of the rubberman" just didn't have the same ring to it as "the rubberman strikes back." Readers will also recall that the word "coup d'état" and not "counterattacks" was the first word used to refer to the book's unique form of civil disobedience—it's only later that Jihye revises the term to "prank" and then finally to "counterattack."

---

* Korean age starts at one and increases every Lunar New Year. Because of this, English speakers would actually consider Jihye to be twenty-nine or even twenty-eight years of age. Another interesting consequence of this age system is that milestones come relatively quicker for Koreans. For example, women in Korea have traditionally been pressured to get married by the age of thirty, which is a young age by today's standards, but even younger when we take into consideration that it is Korean age.

So naturally there was considerable deliberation about whether to retitle the work in English. And while it is ultimately up to marketing to decide the title of a work, I suggested several alternatives for their consideration: *Coup, The Coup, Coup at Thirty, The Thirty-Year-Old Intern, Thirty-Year-Old Revolutionary, Revolution at Thirty,* etc. In the end, it was the somewhat ambiguous title that finally won out. And in hindsight, I'm glad it did. While "counterattacks" does not give as immediate an impression as "coup" or "revolution," perhaps that is the point. The form of protest that Jihye and her friends are practicing is not a full-blown protest "in the square," let alone a coup d'état or social revolution; it is a form of barely impolite protest when litigious measures would have been more than called for, a tamed response to the shameless corruption and exploitation of the powerful, a mere feather on the lopsided scales of (in)justice, a much belated counterpunch by a group of seemingly powerless individuals. Thus, to feel somewhat ambivalent about the title, and by extension to feel frustrated at the banality of the characters' transgressions against the establishment, is to identify with the book's frustrated main character, a woman questioning whether such small acts of dissent can truly make a difference, whether counterattacks can ever be as effective as coups and revolutions.

Readers will also notice that I've done more than my fair share of glossing in this translation, giving brief explanations to wordplay that couldn't be rendered in English without losing its specificity to the Korean experience, as well as providing insights to the idiosyncrasies of life as a Korean office worker. Of course, many references can be omitted without taking away from the overall work, even if doing so might make a particular scene hard to follow. Likewise, rough equivalents can be found in English to create a smoother reading experience. But when every page is a nonstop stream of commentary on the absurdities of Korean society like *C.A.T.*'s pages are, to translate the book without attempting to explain its specificities would be like handing someone your phone and then telling them the wrong password.

It is precisely this cultural subtext that makes *C.A.T.* such a challenging yet rewarding text to read and translate. The book's main themes of injustice and social change will of course be recognized by all readers. After all, is there a country out there that doesn't suffer from political corruption and capitalist exploitation? But understanding why and how Korea is particularly troubled in these aspects is crucial to appreciating the book's many layers. With a Google search, for example, readers will understand that the president referenced on the first page is Roh Tae-woo. But there's always more to the story. Of course most readers will have heard that South Korea was a de facto dictatorship until the late '80s and early '90s. But while the transition to a democracy has improved the country's politics, the fact remains that South Korea is still a frailly young democracy suffering from the vestiges of decades of self-serving leaders. That is why Park Geun-hye, South Korea's eleventh president and daughter to its longest reigning dictator, was impeached in 2017 (the same year *C.A.T.* was published) on charges of influence peddling. When you understand this, you understand exactly why Jihye says on the second page that the world has "taken a few steps in the right direction—*but only a few.*"

The absurdities of South Korea's toxic work culture are also hard to fully grasp without knowledge external to the text. Of course we've all heard about, if not experienced firsthand, the horrors of working for a sexist and exploitive boss like Dept. Head

Kim. I also know my millennial friends will recognize Jihye's attitude in the chapter "Minimal Worker" as a form of quiet quitting. But just like America's endemic workaholism can be traced back to its puritan Calvinist heritage and a mythos of self-determination, Korea's work culture is also the result of a unique history. For example, the idea that leaving work on time is leaving work early is (in part) a remnant of Korean's grueling industrialization period, when people were expected to work longer than physically possible to show to others that they were sacrificing themselves for national causes. And when you understand that South Korea transitioned from third-world country to pop-culture icon in the span of just one generation, you understand exactly why Jihye finds it so difficult to relate to the older employees at the office.

So, what *is* the solution? How do we bring about meaningful change?

While South Korea does have a strong track record of marching for social change—especially when the people come together for a single cause like during the Candlelight Demonstrations of 2016—I understand why Jihye feels disillusioned with these large protests. I used to live near Gwanghwamun Square, and if you've ever been around there on a weekend or holiday, you'll know that protestors are always marching through the streets with loud music and waving flags. If it was a cause I supported, I would sometimes show my solidarity with a low-altitude fist pump, but most of the time, I would stand at the window of my apartment and stare out at the crowds, thinking to myself, "What now?" When people march on the capital with the same frequency as a biweekly book club, it becomes easy to tune the noise out.

Likewise, in a country where maintaining appearances and

kowtowing to authority is the modus operandi, perhaps it's true that miniature protests of impropriety get the ball rolling. But I also understand Jihye's doubt about the long-term effectiveness of leaving insulting letters on your boss's desk or egging shameless politicians. Public humiliation has its place, but like Jihye, most want and need more.

Given these doubts, it's no surprise that Jihye and her friends eventually go their separate ways. Jihye organizes an open-mic event in the park, Gyuok embarks on a journey of self-discovery, Muin finally publishes a webtoon, and Mr. Nam quits mukbangs and opens his own restaurant. So if the book is saying anything, it is that there is no one solution. Change can be as big as joining a movement, or as small as engaging with art, so long as you do *something*.

Sean Lin Halbert
August 2024, Seoul

Here ends Won-pyung Sohn's
Counterattacks at Thirty.

The first edition of this book was printed
and bound at Lakeside Book Company
in Harrisonburg, Virginia, February 2025.

A NOTE ON THE TYPE

The text of this novel was set in Mercury Text G2, a type-face designed by Jonathan Hoefler and Tobias Frere-Jones in 2000. Designer Alexander Isley asked them to explore a text-size variation of Hoefler's Mercury Display font for the *New Times* newspaper chain. The Mercury Text family was the result; designed in a series of grades, every member of the family differs in degrees of darkness on the page while sharing the same foundational geometry. Loosely inspired by Johanna Michael Fleischman's (1701–1768) baroque typefaces, the Mercury Text family draws on Hoefler's penchant for interpreting old type-faces in expressive and elegant ways.

HARPERVIA

An imprint dedicated to publishing international voices,
offering readers a chance to encounter other lives and other
points of view via the language of the imagination.